Fools' Frontier

Crossing the Red Man River when it was in full flood wasn't the wisest thing gambler Duke Benedict and his cowboy sidekick Hank Brazos had ever done. And when the ferry they riding tore free of its ropes, they found themselves driven downstream until their wild ride ended on the banks of Peaceful Valley. Here, a religious order had built itself a town … but the Devil had settled in those parts, too, for one of the townsfolk had just been murdered, and the two new-comers quickly found themselves accused of the killing!

As if that wasn't bad enough, Peaceful Valley was about to get a visit from bad man Chad Irons and his gang of cutthroats. Before he'd been sent to prison, the valley had been Irons' hideaway. Now he intended to take it back – and kill everyone who stood in his way!

One way or another, it was time for Benedict and Brazos to start fighting back …

Fools' Frontier

E. Jefferson Clay

A Black Horse Western

ROBERT HALE

First published by Cleveland Publishing Co. Pty Ltd,
New South Wales, Australia
First published in 1967
© 2020 Mike Stotter and David Whitehead

This edition © The Crowood Press, 2020

ISBN 978 0 7198 3132 4

The Crowood Press
The Stable Block
Crowood Lane
Ramsbury
Marlborough
Wiltshire SN8 2HR

www.bhwesterns.com

Robert Hale is an imprint
of The Crowood Press

Typeset by
Simon and Sons ITES Services Pvt Ltd
Printed and bound in Great Britain by
4Bind Ltd, Stevenage, SG1 2XT

ONE

ONE DEAD
BROTHER

It was mid-morning in Peaceful Valley and all the Brethren who had lived and worked for the Lord in this remote part of Nevada were dutifully going about their daily chores, secure in the knowledge that prayer and good works would ultimately gain them their rightful place in the kingdom of the Master they served so well.

All except two ...

A mile west of the little mine that supplied the Brethren with the gold to fashion their chalices and statues of worship, Brother Smoke was hard at work fashioning a hole in a secluded glade ... and a puzzled Brother Jackson was approaching through aspen and birch, drawn by the sounds of digging.

Brother Smoke, a big, powerful man with hard, dark eyes and a black spade beard, worked swiftly and efficiently. It was hot. Sweat coursed from his pores and made the black cassock cling to his back. But he didn't mind; as foreman of the Brethren who worked the Paradise Mine, he was accustomed to hard labor.

Finally the hole was deep enough. He set down the shovel and smiled as he hefted the canvas sack. Two hundred dollars' worth of gold at least, likely more, a nice addition to what he had already buried.

Suddenly Brother Smoke froze.

A dark shadow had fallen across the hole.

His big head jerked around and he looked into a familiar face.

The man stared at the sack in Smoke's hand with an expression of total astonishment on his face.

"Jackson!" Smoke breathed, coming slowly erect.

Jackson's eyes lifted from the sack and focused accusingly on Smoke's bearded face. "Is what I see with my eyes what it seems to be? Thou art stealing Brethren gold?"

"Stealin'?" Smoke's cunning brain worked at desperate speed. Somehow he found a smile. "Brother Jackson, do you really believe a member of the Brethren would steal—*could* steal?"

A flicker of uncertainty crossed Jackson's lean face. A founding member of the Brethren and a man of absolute virtue, he always found it difficult to suspect evil in other men. Yet everything he saw here pointed to guilt, he told himself. However, he must at least grant his brother a chance to explain.

"If thou art not caught in theft, Brother Smoke," he said, using the biblical idiom of the Upper Brethren, "then what art thou doing?"

6

"I didn't wish for a single Brethren to know of this until the day, Brother," Smoke said with convincing regret. "But now that you have seen what I'm about, I have no choice but to reveal my secret."

"Secret, Brother? And what is this day thou speaketh of?"

"Why, Thanksgivin', of course. You know what store the Deacon sets by that feast, Brother. Well, I ... I wanted to do somethin' really special for him ... you know, to repay him for all he's done for me." Smoke licked his lips, and then, growing more assured by the second, went on quickly, "The truth of it is, Brother Jackson, I'm makin' the Deacon a statue of Saint Jude—gonna be the finest statue we got in Redemption. Mebbe it was wrong of me, knowin' the Deacon's rules about the gold and all, but there was no other way I could make the statue in secret without takin' the gold from the mine." He reached out to touch Jackson's black-garbed arm. "If I done wrong, it was only because I hold the Deacon so high, Brother. You understand, don't you? Tell me I ain't done wrong, Brother."

As Brother Jackson looked into Smoke's pleading, dark eyes, he felt his uncertainty begin to ebb. "Well, Brother Smoke, this is most irregular ... and I'm sure I don't know what the Deacon would say, but ..." He paused. "I shall be honest with thee, Brother. Thy explanation has the ring of truth, but a canker of doubt remains in my heart. Perhaps if I could see some evidence of your statue ... Are you using a mold?"

"Mold? Why, yeah, of course." Smoke turned and gestured in the direction of Red Man River. "My mold's in one of them caves by the river, not far from here. We can …"

Brother Smoke broke off and swabbed at his eyes with his sleeve, then he hung his head. "I … I'm sorry, Brother," he muttered. "I—it just hit me that … that you really thought I was stealin'. I guess I can't really blame you, but it's a hard thing all the same. I mean, I know I'm kind of a hard case compared to you Upper Brethren, but I try my best to …"

"Brother, say not another word," Jackson implored, his face flooding with forgiveness and contrition as he put an arm around the big man's shoulders. "I see now the wrong I have done thee. Thou art a true Brethren and I know thy innocence. Come, compose thyself, my Brother, and tell me that thou forgiveth my injustice."

Smoke squeezed Jackson's arm. "Brother, I knew you couldn't really mean it. I knew it."

Jackson's eyes were misty. "Then say thou forgiveth me, Brother. Put it in words."

"I forgive you," Smoke said magnanimously,

Brother Jackson beamed happily as he took the sack of gold from Smoke's hand. "Then it is between us as before. Now let us go to the caves."

"Lead the way, Brother."

Jackson turned and strode off, Smoke lumbering behind and scanning the forest in all directions. Seeing that no one was in sight, he moved forward on suddenly quickened feet. Then, as deftly as a child slipping a ribbon over the neck of a kitten, he looped the rope cincture from his waist around Jackson's neck and snapped it tight with all his strength.

Brother Jackson's body jerked convulsively, but Smoke held him fast against him until his body went slack.

"Hallelujah, Brother," he panted, slinging the rope's end over a low tree branch. Then he watched the purple faced corpse swing and said, "Amen."

"I tell you I already got a woman," big Hank Brazos lied to the mountain of female flesh.

"Ah, but not such a woman like Pandora, eh, Caballero?"

"Well, mebbe she ain't quite so well nourished up as you, ma'am. But she's plenty bossy and she sure don't take kindly to me messin' with other women."

"Pah!" Pandora placed a plump hand on an enormous hip. "Gringo women, pah! They have no fire, no stomachs. Spanish women have much passion and tenderness. When we make love, a hombre knows he is with a woman, not some skinny little mouse."

Some women chattering nearby began to laugh and the cheeks of the blond young giant in the faded purple shirt, colored through his dark tan. Brazos was cursing himself for getting entangled with this mountainous female. Following a long trail with his partner, Duke Benedict, he had ridden all night; then reaching the wagon camp at sunrise, he'd been pressed to stay for breakfast by Pandora. The meal had been top class; frijoles, Mexican beans, tortillas and the best coffee he'd tasted in a long time.

Now it seemed a price was to be paid.

9

Mustering a boyish grin, he tried to explain one more time that he had business in another direction that kept him from accepting her generous offer to let him drive her wagon the rest of the way to Colorado, even if she was prepared to feed him like a king on delicious Mexican food every mile.

"You see, my pard and I are lookin' for a feller, ma'am," he said, glancing around in vain for some sign of Duke Benedict. "But I appreciate your offer, and if I was lookin' for a woman I sure enough wouldn't have to look no further than you."

Pandora was unimpressed. A surfeit of rich cooking and a lack of sleep had resulted in her last driver taking flight two days ago, and this big gringo with the bashful grin and big muscles looked strong enough to drive a Conestoga clear to Washington.

"You do not want to look for feller," she assured him, simpering and reaching for him with a hand the size of a supper plate. "You will be happy with Pandora."

It was no time for chivalry. Hank Brazos ducked under her pudgy arm and bolted—head-first into the belly of the biggest Mexican he'd ever seen in his life.

"Uh … 'scuse me," he said politely enough, straightening his battered hat. "Kinda in a hurry, so if you'll—"

"Uno momento, compadre," growled the Mexican heavyweight, taking a white bone toothpick from greasy lips. His face was pocked and seamed and the black patch he wore over one eye made him look like a baby-killer on a bad day. "I am Manuel Vadinho, the wagon master of this train." He inclined his head at Pandora who was standing behind Brazos with hands on massive hips looking thunderous and hurt at the same time. "You were not polite just now to my sister, señor."

"Your sister?"

"Si, my little baby sister whom I treasure."

Brazos turned his young, sun-bronzed face to the sky. She *would* have a brother. And he *would* dress out at about two eighty pounds of prime Mexican beef.

Brazos pulled his mouth into a grin. "Okay, señor, if you hold as how I was impolite, then you got my apology." He turned and nodded to the scowling Pandora. "Sorry, ma'am."

Pandora grunted and her brother nodded in approval.

"Well spoken, gringo, you have breeding." Vadinho smiled. "And now you will resume your conversation with my sister."

Brazos' forced grin faded. The big Mex wasn't asking, he was telling. Brazos looked past him and saw that silent men were gathering about. They'd looked friendly at breakfast. They didn't look friendly now.

A faint bell of warning rang in his brain. Where the hell had Benedict got to, anyway? His stare went past the group of men but all he saw were their horses and his big dog Bullpup chomping on a beef shank.

He turned back to Vadinho. "'Tweren't rightly a conversation we was havin', señor. Your sister offered me a job drivin' her wagon and I had to turn her down."

The Mexican's solitary black eye glittered.

"Señor," he said deliberately, "you do not understand. We *need* another driver."

Mental agility wasn't Hank Brazos' long suit, but suddenly he understood why they'd been so anxious for him and Benedict to stop off and share breakfast with them. Along the Galveston waterfront, they called it shanghaiing.

"Señor," he said softly, "you're startin' to crowd me and that surely is somethin' I can't abide. Step aside—I'm leavin'."

But a heavy hand fell on Brazos' forearm as he made to step past.

"You will remain, gringo," Vadinho hissed.

Brazos exploded.

He looped a right into the big Mexican's belly and saw his mouth balloon with sudden air. Vadinho was all meat and no bones. His ornamental sombrero flew from his head as he jack-knifed forward. Brazos seized the back of his jacket and jerked his head down to uppercut him in the face with his knee.

Vadinho's proud Mexican beak was flattened, but instead of going backwards as Brazos expected, he grabbed at the Texan and butted him in the belly in blind panic. Brazos seized his arms, fell backwards to the ground and then, shoving a big boot in the Mexican's guts, threw him ten feet against the mirror of a bureau that had been offloaded from Mrs. Storey's wagon while they fixed a broken axle.

Brazos winced as glass burst, furniture splintered and Vadinho threshed amongst the debris as his sister screamed.

Then Brazos had other things to occupy him as the others came in with a rush.

The sight of Vadinho staggering past leaking blood succeeded in claiming Duke Benedict's attention. Nothing less could have done it, for when the ruckus began Hank Brazos' tall, good-looking partner was sitting in elegant splendor in the wagon of the widow Schaefer who had just displayed excellent taste by saying that never in her life had she met a man half as handsome. That was the sort of dialogue the gambling man loved to hear, particularly from somebody with an hour-glass figure, magnificent red hair and the most spectacular bosom in Nevada. Regretfully doffing his hat to the widow and thanking her for her hospitality, Benedict stepped outside just in time to see Brazos flatten a lumbering Swede with a blow that would have felled an ox, and then evade the clutching hands of a dozen angry-looking men who came leaping towards him.

"Let's get the hell outa here, Benedict," Brazos roared as a lump of two-by-one wagon slat came flying after him. "Pronto!"

Duke Benedict needed only one glance to realize what was going on. He'd been propelled into too many wild, bone-cracking brawls by his big, illiterate trail partner in the past not to know the ropes. So he doffed his hat once more to the widow as Brazos pounded past, then he sprinted after him.

That was when an enjoyable brawl turned into something else. Getting up off the ground after a Brazos haymaker had smashed his nose, a red-headed teamster lurched upright with a gun in his fist and fired.

The bullet went six feet too high. Duke Benedict's reaction was that of a man as skilled with a gun as he was with a deck of cards. As wild-eyed wagoners threw themselves left and right out of the line of fire, he spun, lifted his right-hand gun clear and shot the smoking Colt .45 from the wagoner's hand.

The gun was what he aimed for, but by chance the slug ricocheted up, furrowed the side of the redhead's temple and knocked him down as if he'd been pole axed.

Benedict had played the gunsmoke game too often not to know that the redhead was only creased. In the stunned moments of silence that followed the blast of guns he tried to say as much, but didn't get far. Shock turned to rage on the faces of Brazos' adversaries. A fat man bellowed, "Get your guns, he's murdered Slim!" and there was a wild rush for the wagons.

If they'd had any doubts about whether they should make dust or not, Brazos and Benedict didn't have any now. Luckily the horses weren't far away. Benedict hit leather first and then Brazos bounded into the saddle of his appaloosa a moment later. Both left the scene at a storming gallop, with Bullpup streaking at their heels.

Riding low in their saddles, they zigzagged the horses as guns started to roar behind. But the wagoners' aims were poor, and soon they were out of range, pounding west along the deep-rutted wagon trail.

"You all right?" Benedict asked.

"'Course I am. I was goin' great until you beefed that joker. Why'd you have to do a fool thing like that?"

The fact that the man was no worse than creased had nothing to do with the swift fury that leaped into Benedict's eyes. It was the big Texan's ingratitude that galled.

"You cretin!" Benedict barked, ducking his head as he sped beneath a low branch. "They were about to pound you into the gravel when I bought in. Next time I'll let them go right ahead."

"That mightn't be too long."

"What?"

Brazos jerked a thumb over his shoulder. Hipping around in the saddle, Benedict looked backtrail to see that four rifle-toting riders had burst away from the wagon train and were drumming after them in swift pursuit.

The look Benedict directed at his trail partner would have peeled paint. At times like this he was prone to bitter reflection on the irony of how a gambling man of quality and breeding like himself came to be riding with an over-muscled, illiterate saddle bum with a talent for stirring up trouble second to none.

Sometimes he almost enjoyed the luxury of letting his thoughts run along those superior lines, but not today—not with a lynch-minded posse hard on their heels.

TWO

THE WILD WAY
SOUTH

They rode west for several miles. First the hills crowded them on either side, then they swept down to broad, flat country where the timber thinned out, giving way to big granite boulders that stood high above the yellow summer grass. The boulders, red and yellow and scarred with age and weather, looked ancient and solemn, like tombstones in a church-yard. At another time, Benedict's curiosity would have demanded that he pull up and study the strange formations at close quarters, but there was a cloud of dust behind them, and not too far behind at that.

They galloped across the flats and over a sea of red flowers, then through a tall stand of cotton-woods from which red-wing blackbirds rose in a flock, shrieking at being disturbed.

A mile farther on the way led past a lake. Heavy cedars stood along the banks in clusters. Between the trees and the water's edge bloomed brilliant yellow cactus flowers, their vivid color mirrored in the glassy surface.

"Pretty country!" Brazos shouted as they left the lake behind, but this drew no response from a sullen Duke Benedict.

The horses swept over a knoll and went racing through a stand of tall cat-tail grass whose stalks whipped at them. The sun was getting hot. Bullpup's tongue hung out four inches and the horses were sweat-foamed as they struggled up a steep ridge. Then Red Man River lay below.

"Judas!" Brazos grunted, sawing the appaloosa to a halt. "Look at that!"

Benedict stared and tense lines appeared in his face. He and Brazos had known that Red Man River was located some five miles from the wagon camp and they'd calculated that the posse would likely quit there. But nature had played a joker. The Red Man was flooded. Normally a shallow stream snaking through the looming Sourdough Mountains, the Red Man that morning was a broad, angry red torrent. Melting snows in the north had been flowing into the river for a week, then heavy rain in the hills twenty-four hours ago had lifted its level almost to its banks. It was an ominous sight with its yellow flood froth and the speeding deadfall logs bobbing on its surface ... almost as ominous as the dust cloud behind them.

It was a bad moment, but then Benedict spotted a rooftop through the river willows along the bank almost directly ahead, and beyond the roof was the prow of a boat.

"Could be the ferry we heard about in Oxbend!" Benedict said, pointing.

"It better be," Brazos replied grimly as a fast glance over his shoulder revealed the fast-moving horsemen visible now at the base of the column of hoof-kicked dust. He touched spur to flank and led the way down the ridge at a dead run.

Five minutes later they were reining in by the building on the river shore. It was a ferry station cum general store built up on stout logs to keep it out of the reach of floods like this one. And there *was* a ferry boat.

The ferryman came out as they swung down, but they were more interested in the boat. It was a rough looking craft, unpainted and weathered, but it looked solid enough. Brazos, who'd had a little more experience with boats than Benedict, saw that it was a keel boat converted to a horse and passenger ferry by adding a sloping loading ramp to the stern and a horse stall by the cabin. It had two big pulleys fore and aft through which a stout rope ran from a willow on the store side to a big cottonwood across the river.

"What do you think?" Benedict said, looking at the way the water swirled about the boat.

"I think we got no choice," Brazos said with rough logic. He seized the lines of Benedict's horse, then whistled to Bullpup who stood off, his eyes rolling in alarm as he looked at the Red Man. "You fix the geezer up while I load the horses," Brazos added.

Benedict walked towards the station as the ferryman, a pop-eyed, rough-looking man with a great thatch of frizzy hair, jumped down from the landing and ran their way.

"Hey, what the hell you think you're doin'?" he bellowed.

"What's it goddamn look like?" retorted Brazos, forcing the reluctant horses onto the jetty.

"The ferry's closed," the man shouted. "Any idjut could see you can't use it when the water's up like this."

But Brazos paid him no heed. The man let out a string of curses and started towards the huge Texan. But Benedict blocked his way and pulled out a leather billfold.

"We don't have any choice but to take your boat across, friend," he said, producing money. "How much?"

"Blast you, I tell you my boat ain't for hire. You try to take her across today and you'll likely get washed down Blackwater Gorge, and nobody ain't ever come outa there alive."

"Five dollars," Benedict said, thrusting bills into the ferryman's shirt pocket. "That's double a fair price."

"It ain't for hire," the ferryman roared, red-faced with rage as he plucked the money out and threw it in Benedict's face. "I ain't riskin' my boat for no—"

There was a swift blur of movement, a thud, a startled grunt, and before the last note had fluttered to the ground, the ferryman was already there, stretched out, with a rising lump on his ugly forehead.

"I told you we have no choice, my rock-headed friend," Benedict muttered. Then, holstering his gun, he leaped onto the jetty and jumped to the deck as Brazos drove the long barge pole into the sand with all his power and sent the boat driving away from the shore.

The ferry shuddered and gave a protesting groan of its timbers when the full force of the current hit the gunwales. On Brazos' instructions, Benedict seized the rope and pulled hard, hand over hand, as the bigger man discarded the pole and worked the big oar mounted by the tiller.

Thrusting their way towards the middle of the river, with the horses whickering and stamping in the box as the boat rocked violently, they didn't have much time for anything but their labors. But they did note the yawning stone jaws of Blackwater Gorge a mile south, through which the boiling river ran. It wasn't a comforting sight—nor was the cluster of riders who suddenly burst into view on the ridge they'd vacated just minutes before.

"Faster, Yank!" Brazos shouted, his faded purple shirt already sticking to his Herculean frame from the sweat of his exertions. "We ain't outa range of the bank yet!"

Duke Benedict considered physical labor of any kind beneath his dignity, but he worked like a roust-about over the next hectic minutes as the posse men flailed their mounts towards the river.

The boat reached the half-way point with the rope bowed far downstream and stretched tight. Now they were working at an angle slightly against the river and the boat slowed dramatically. Above the roar of the river, they heard hoof beats and angry shouts. They jerked their heads around and saw their pursuers massed on the bank by the boathouse. Then a shot rang out and lead slashed into the water.

Benedict drew his Colt and sent three high shots blasting back. Posse men dived left and right, but then Vadinho, a wild look of inspiration on his evil face, jumped at the straining rope with an uplifted machete.

Benedict drilled a shot at the huge Mexican, but the motion of the boat ruined his aim. Sunlight flashed on the descending blade, there was the thud of contact, and then a wildly whipping serpent of rope rose high in the air and hummed through the pulleys.

It took Benedict and Brazos a stunned moment to fully realize what had happened. Then they grasped at the rope together. Desperately Brazos tried to knot it over a pulley post, but now the boat was rushing downstream crazily and the rope burned over his fingers and was gone.

Benedict grabbed the tiller and reefed at it with all his strength, but to no avail. Shouldering him aside, a grim-jawed Brazos seized the handle and heaved against it, huge slabs of muscle writhing beneath his shirt.

The boat kept right on going downstream. Red Man River had it completely in its deadly grip now, and it was a power no man could stand against. They were helpless.

"Adios, señor gringos!"

They looked bleak-eyed back towards the swiftly-receding ferry house. Their last glimpse of an exultant Vadinho saw him standing on the jetty waving goodbye with the machete, his teeth flashing in the sun.

Then they were hanging on tight as the Red Man narrowed and the boat was whipped below the towering walls of Blackwater Gorge.

"Ass backwards into hell!" Hank Brazos gritted, clutching for dear life to the horse box as the boat sped stern-first down the gorge. "What a way to go!"

"And whose fault is that?" a crouching Benedict snarled through a white wall of spray. "Who was the moron who got into trouble with that overfed Mexican strumpet in the first—"

Benedict's voice was cut off by a shuddering crunch as the keel clipped a submerged rock. The boat canted on its side and almost threw him into the water. From the horse box came a scream of terror and a crash. Forgetting his own plight, Brazos threw himself through the doorway. Benedict's black had fallen and was lashing wildly about. Thrusting his battered, rolling-eyed appaloosa aside with a powerful shoulder, the big man seized the downed horse by the head harness and tried to heave it upright. The panic-stricken black screamed and a hoof glanced off Brazos. He cursed feelingly and cried out:

"Gimme a hand with these horses afore they cripple theirselves, goddammit!"

Duke Benedict stayed right where he was. He liked his horse but he dearly loved life, and his hold on that precious commodity had never seemed so tenuous.

Mouthing curses at fat Mexican tortilla eaters and dandy gambling men plus rain, flood and rapids, Brazos somehow managed to get the black horse back on its feet. As he did, the keel glanced off another rock and the boat shuddered, then swung around to spear prow-first into a deeper, smoother stretch of the river. Brazos remained with the horses until they grew calmer, then he staggered from the box to peer ahead.

They were no longer travelling backwards, but it didn't cheer Hank Brazos much. He was still sure they were going to hell.

So was Benedict as he hung on for dear life and watched the towering black cliffs rush past. Benedict was surprised. Not because he was certain he'd die— he'd lived cheek-by-jowl with Old Man Death too long for that—but because of the manner of the death confronting him. Drowned on a ferry boat in an obscure backwater of Nevada? It was a hell of a note. A reckless gambler, gunfighter, adventurer and romancer who just couldn't keep out of trouble with women, he'd sometimes conceded the possibility of going down in a saloon gunfight, or of being shot in the back by an enraged husband.

But drowned in a dirty river? Never. It simply wasn't a suitable end for Duke Benedict.

Lacking Benedict's imagination, Hank Brazos wasn't thinking of how he'd prefer to go. What really crushed him was his feeling of total helplessness. A man of uncommon physical power, he felt a puny weakling in the river's roaring grip. If he cursed one thing more than another as he waited for the final crash that would spell oblivion, it was Lady Luck's capriciousness in flooding the Red Man on this lousy day of all days. What Brazos didn't understand was the fact that it was only because the Red Man *was* flooded that they'd survived this long. At normal depth, the rapids of Blackwater Canyon would have ground the craft to matchwood within seconds. But, running ten feet above its normal height, the Red Man, clear of most jagged rocks, raced the boat along on its roaring current and then suddenly spewed it, battered and holed but still afloat, from the stone jaws of the gorge.

It was the sudden lessening of the deafening roar that first penetrated the senses of the two men. Dazedly they lifted sodden heads and then naked sunlight fell upon them for the first time in almost an hour. The boat was still held in the grip of the current, but now they saw trees, green grass and shelving slopes of sand on either side.

It had been a long time since Duke Benedict had said a prayer of thanksgiving, but his lips were moving as he found he could stand upright without being hurled to the deck again. He turned to Brazos and their eyes flashed a look of understanding they would never put into words: they might fight a lot of the time, but together they were lucky and they'd never been luckier than today—

Then the moment passed and things returned to normal with Benedict's dark frown. "Well, don't just stand there, Brazos. Give me a hand with the damned tiller."

Brazos didn't snap back, mainly because he was too happy to be alive. Leaping to the bow, he gripped the handle and gave it a mighty wrench. Half-filled with water now, the boat answered sluggishly and, yellow water streaming from its prow, angled towards the eastern shore. Moments later the hull ground into the soft sand.

Brazos heaved a giant sigh. "Man ... you ever seen anythin' as purty as that, Yank?"

"I don't believe I have, Reb."

It was half an hour later and the two men stood beside their horses atop a green ridge a quarter mile east of the river. Below them the battered boat lay on a strip of yellow sand like a beached whale. The sun had dried them out, and now, apart from lumps, bruises, and legs that were still somewhat shaky, they were little the worse for their ordeal. The horses, however, had been badly knocked about and wouldn't be fit to ride for some days. But Bullpup had recovered completely and was running around in circles sniffing at everything with tail-wagging delight. Every now and then he looked back at the Red Man to growl and show that he'd never been *really* scared at all.

From the ridge the men looked out over a deep valley of incredible beauty. Cupped on three sides by the lofty, tree-covered slopes of the towering Sourdough Mountains, the valley, bathed in brilliant sunshine, was all green and gold. Its air of tranquility was almost tangible.

A mile or so due west stood a small town dominated by a big, white-painted church with a high steeple. They could make out the figures of men, women and children on the streets. A pony herd grazed on flower-dotted grasses along a little creek that wound down out of the mountains to the Red Man. Goats, sheep and cattle fed on other pastures.

The eye-pleasing scenery was in sharp contrast to the rough-and-ready country they'd just come through north of Blackwater Gorge. Here was solitude and silence in a haven of lush grass, birch, pine, aspen, cedar and willow, ringed by rock and water and high blue sky.

"You know," Brazos said grudgingly after a long silence, "this almost beats Texas, danged if it don't."

"Everything beats Texas," Boston-born Benedict replied automatically. Then, frowning: "You hear anything about this place when we were up north?"

Brazos shook his head. "Nary a word." He scratched his neck as he scanned the mountains and the river. "Some hideaway, huh? Say, I wonder if …"

"If what?"

"Well, this is just the sort of place Bo Rangle might pick to hide out in—if he ever found it."

At Brazos' mention of the man they'd hunted for so long, Duke Benedict's handsome face darkened, then his mind went back to the dying days of the Civil War and a place called Pea Ridge, Georgia. There, on a day never to be forgotten, Union and Confederate troops had fought a bloody battle for a shipment of Confederate gold, but in the end the gold was snatched away by the infamous Rangle's Raiders. Rebel Sergeant Hank Brazos and Federal Captain Duke Benedict, the sole survivors of one hundred and fifty men, had been brought together by chance at war's end, and now they hunted Rangle and the gold for which so many brave men had died. Benedict and Brazos, coming from vastly different backgrounds, disagreed on just about everything under the sun, but somehow their partnership worked. They'd dogged Rangle's trail over a thousand violent miles. They knew him to be somewhere in Nevada, but Benedict didn't believe he could have stumbled onto this hidden valley, and he told Brazos so.

"Yeah, mebbe you're right," Brazos conceded. "Anyway, let's go take a look at that town yonder. I'm curious to find out what kinda folks live there, so hell and gone from the rest of the world."

They set off through golden aspen, leading the horses. After travelling no more than two hundred yards, Brazos suddenly stopped and peered about.

"What's wrong?" Benedict asked.

"Bullpup. Where is he?"

Benedict glanced around but saw no sign of Brazos' ubiquitous monster dog. "Most probably after a rabbit," he decided.

Brazos put fingers to his teeth and whistled. But there was no response. "That's mighty curious," he muttered, broad face showing concern. He pulled his horse's head around. "We'll have to find him, Yank."

"Leave him," Benedict said impatiently. "He'll catch up."

"I'd sooner leave you," Brazos growled, and with his horse's lines looped over his arm, started back.

Benedict hesitated for a long moment, then sighed in resignation and followed, tramping back through the groves and slopes, with Brazos stopping every few paces to whistle. Then they heard the unmistakable sound of Bullpup's bark, somewhere off to the right.

Brazos stiffened and his hand went to his gun. "Somethin's wrong, Yank. I know that bark."

"My guess would be that he's been bailed up by a chipmunk."

Brazos frowned. "Mind the horses while I take a look."

Benedict protested, but found himself holding both horses anyway as Brazos tramped up the slope, massive shoulders straining against the faded purple shirt. The big man vanished into the brush and Benedict puffed impatiently on his cigar. A few minutes passed before Brazos suddenly appeared, looking grim.

"Yank, tether the hosses and get up here—quick."

Benedict tied the horses to a stunted dogwood and climbed the slope. Bullpup was still barking as Benedict pushed his way through a screen of flowering brush and came to a dead halt, an involuntary exclamation breaking from his lips.

Twenty feet away, in the middle of a grassy clearing, a skinny man in the long black cassock of a monk was turning slowly on the end of a yellow rope knotted around the branch of a tree.

"Good grief," Benedict said after a handful of seconds.

Brazos drew his Bowie knife to cut the man down.

The party of black-garbed Brethren riders were searching for the missing Brother Jackson near the river when they heard the distant barks of a dog. Reining in, they keened their ears. Brother Miller's hearing was not as sharp as it had been, but he knew dogs. This one, he decided, had a note of alarm in his bark.

"We shall investigate, Brothers," he decided, and kneed his horse into a trot.

They'd closed the staring eyes and gaping mouth, but the face of the dead man still reflected the shock and terror he'd felt as he was hurled into eternity.

"Incredible," Benedict murmured, looking about him. "I've never seen a more beautiful, peaceful looking—"

Benedict cut himself short at the sound of thudding hoofs. Exchanging a glance, the two men drew six-guns and got to their feet as Bullpup let out a warning growl. They were standing over the corpse, guns at the ready, when a dozen men wearing the same black garb as the dead man, rode into the clearing.

The men reined up sharply, alarmed. Then they saw the figure stretched out in the deep grass and their alarm turned to horror.

"Brother Jackson?" gasped portly Brother Tucker. Ignoring the implied threat of naked guns, he stepped down from the saddle and started forward, no vestige of color in his normally ruddy face.

Duke Benedict slowly lowered his gun as the fat man knelt by the corpse. None of the strangely-garbed men wore guns. He said, "We just came upon this man's body, friend. He was hanging from that bough."

"On the end of this," added Brazos, holding the cincture high.

"Murdered," breathed Brother Miller, sliding from the saddle. Shock faded and a suspicion entered his eyes as he turned to face Benedict and Brazos. "Who art thou, strangers? And how do thee come to be in Peaceful Valley?"

Uncomfortably aware of the heavily speculative stares of every man now, Benedict told them as briefly as he could of the events of the past four hours. There was no telling what the Brethren thought of the story, but when Benedict was through, Miller excused himself, then drew his men aside to confer out of earshot.

Finally Miller came back to where the two tall men waited impatiently. The Brother's voice was toneless as he said:

"Strangers, we do believe what thou telleth us, but because the death of a Brother is involved here, we

30

feel we must ask thee to return with us to Redemption and repeat thy story to the Deacon?"

"The Deacon?" Brazos said.

"Our holy pastor," Miller explained. He looked at Benedict. "Well, what sayest thou, stranger?"

"I say no," was Benedict's quick reply.

"Hey now, just a minute, Yank," Brazos protested. "They ain't askin' much. And these fellers are men of God. They ain't gonna pull nothin' sneaky on us."

"The big brother speaketh with wisdom," declared Brother Miller. He looked at Benedict. "Well?"

Furrows appeared in Benedict's broad forehead as he pondered the situation. "Very well," he said finally. "But I'm not as trusting as my partner. I have seen things done under the name of religion that would curdle the milk of a snake." He housed his gun. "We'll come with you, but only to clear up any doubt about our innocence. If you men show so much as one flicker of treachery or violence, you will surely have more than one dead man on your hands."

Brother Miller gave a small bow of acknowledgment. "So be it." He turned to the others. "Very well, my Brothers, place the body of our dear departed Brother Jackson on a horse, and we shall return to the settlement."

Minutes later they set off, Benedict and Brazos grimfaced as they led their horses east, the faces of the Brethren showing nothing. Had any man glanced backwards as the cavalcade moved off, he might have seen the pale oval of a face staring after them from a thicket

THREE

VIOLENCE IN PARADISE

Deacon McCloud was writing Sunday's sermon.

It was a good sermon. All his sermons were. There was an ounce or two of brotherly love in it, a pinch of charity and, in equal parts, dashes of faith, hope, honor for your father and mother, and a warning against coveting your neighbor's wife—or anybody's wife for that matter.

But the main ingredients he lashed into every sermon were hellfire and damnation. That was what they wanted and by God that was what he gave them. There was nothing meek, mild or wishy-washy about the Deacon or his faith. A towering, fierce-eyed giant of a man, he was as capable of hammering the Lord's word home with fists or boots as with words. Nobody snoozed through the Deacon's sermons, not with fire

32

and damnation, plague and pestilence choking up the air.

Satan was the Deacon's mortal enemy, and he fought him for the souls of his faithful followers with a zeal that never diminished. On an illumined panel behind his desk was the legend: LOVE THE LORD. On another was: HATE THE DEVIL.

McCloud had been conscious of the distracting sounds from Peace Street for some moments before he reluctantly put down his big quill pen and rose to go onto the balcony and see what was causing it. Unlike the other male members of the sect that he had founded, the Deacon did not wear the black cassock. His attire included a black frock coat, black trousers, high-heeled black boots, a white shirt and a crimson vest. An uncommonly tall man, he walked with a fluid grace that was a legacy of the violent profession he'd followed before the Lord had called.

Stepping onto the balcony, he saw a growing knot of Brothers and Sisters forming around two tall strangers. Then his gaze riveted on the black-garbed form draped across the big appaloosa horse. He gaped, spun on his heel and hurried to the stairs.

He met Brother Smoke on the stairway.

"Brother," he boomed, "what is going on?"

"It's Brother Jackson, Deacon," Smoke panted, his eyes wild. "He's dead, Deacon. Murdered."

"Murdered?" McCloud was stunned. "Murdered?" he repeated as if he couldn't believe it, then he went down to the street.

Benedict and Brazos, already uneasy, found little that was reassuring in this burning-eyed giant with his flowing, shoulder-length hair and iron jaw. Brazos moved his hand towards his hip, but Benedict grasped his arm.

"Take it easy, Reb. Let's wait and see how they play the game before we draw cards."

Brazos grunted in agreement, then the crowd of black-garbed men and women opened up to leave an avenue for the Deacon to come through.

Dust rose from McCloud's big boots as he came to a halt before the two strangers. The burning eyes ran over them, missing nothing. McCloud noted Brazos' massive shoulders, the suggestion of enormous power in his Herculean body, his guileless but dangerous blue eyes. In Benedict's handsome face he read a razor-sharp intelligence, but his attention was drawn more by the slender, supple hands and the unspoken challenge of the two tied-down Peacemakers on Benedict's slim hips. A strong man and a gunfighter, he thought.

"I am Deacon McCloud," he said. "Who are you men—and why are you here in Peaceful Valley?"

That didn't sound promising, but Benedict didn't let it throw him. Quickly he related the story of their journey through Blackwater Gorge, their arrival in the valley and their subsequent discovery of the dead man.

By the time Benedict was through, the crowd had swollen to about a hundred. McCloud cleared his throat and turned to Brother Miller.

"Is this how it was, Brother Miller?" Unlike the Upper Brethren who had had their own religious sect for years before McCloud came to lead them, the Deacon did not employ the Old Testament "thees" and "thous".

Miller drew the Deacon aside and spoke in a whisper. Both men glanced frequently at Benedict and Brazos. Once McCloud's black eyes flashed, but from then on the Deacon seemed to grow calmer and quieter, and when he finally turned back to them, they were surprised by his gentle tone.

"Brother Benedict and Brother Brazos, you have suffered a cruel and shocking experience. Forgive me if I appeared stern at first, but this tragedy has stricken us all. However, we must not burden weary travelers with our private griefs. You have come far and I observe that your animals and yourselves are in need of rest and refreshment. You will permit us to extend our hospitality?"

Brazos and Benedict were taken by surprise. The Brethren had said little on the ride in but both had been aware of anger and suspicion directed towards them.

"Why, that's mighty white of you, Deacon," Brazos said, relieved, just as a powerfully built man with a black spade beard thrust his way through the throng.

"Deacon, I protest," the bearded man said in a rough voice that belonged to the Lay Brethren. "I've been listenin' to the story these men have been tellin' you and it don't ring right to me. Brother Jackson's been murdered and Brother Miller found these fellers with his body, so it seems to me that—"

"Brother Smoke," McCloud snapped, and if there were any lingering doubts in the minds of the two newcomers as to who was in total charge here, it was dispelled then. "Did I ask you to speak on this matter?"

Smoke went pale. "Sorry, Deacon," he muttered, "it's just that—"

"It is just that you forget yourself at times, Brother," McCloud said. He turned back to Brazos and Benedict. "You will forgive the interruption, Brothers? All of us are overwrought at the moment. But you will accept our hospitality?"

Brazos gave a ready, "Sure will," but Benedict hesitated. Suspicious by nature, he had always been wary of men who held themselves above others. Despite his weariness, he would rather have moved on, but there was a heavy argument against that. Miller had told him that the only way in or out of the valley was by the river trail and that was now under water. Besides, their horses weren't fit to travel and wouldn't be for a few days.

So Benedict reluctantly agreed to stay and McCloud gave a small bow.

"We always give sustenance and shelter to travelers, Brother Benedict," he said, "even though strangers are a great rarity here. Brother Tucker shall see to it that you may bathe, change into fresh clothing and eat heartily. After that you may find it convenient to visit me and furnish me with more details about your discovery of poor Brother Jackson's body."

"Sure we will," said Brazos. "And we appreciate your hospitality, Deacon."

"My pleasure as well as my obligation," replied McCloud. "There is, however, one small thing, Brothers. Your weapons. As you will have observed, no man wears arms in Peaceful Valley. It is one of our inflexible rules. I am sure you will not object to turning your guns over to Brother Tucker when you bathe. They will be held for you until it is time for you to leave."

Again Benedict had reservations, but Brazos, happily anticipating hot suds, a clean shirt and a meal, overrode him.

"We don't mind turnin' over our guns," the big Texan assured McCloud. "Come on, Benedict, drop that hard eyed look and let's get goin'. Right this minute I could eat a bullock and wash it down with ..." Brazos paused at a thought. "Er, Deacon, I don't suppose you people have hard likker here?"

"Sorry, Brother, no."

Brazos managed a grin even if he felt as dry as a corked leg. "Well, I guess a little goin' without never hurt no man," he said, moving towards Brother Tucker who was waiting to lead them away. He paused, with Benedict at his side, and looked back soberly. "I sure hope you can figure out who killed that feller, Deacon."

"I am certain we will, Brother Brazos," McCloud said in a strange tone.

Benedict and Brazos felt just fine. A half-hour's soaking in a hot tub in Brother Tucker's bath-house had soothed their aches and bruises and pumped new strength into weary muscles. The trousers that were a trifle large and the shirt that was a shade small were not the fastidious Benedict's idea of elegant apparel, but he didn't complain. The long bath had eased his weariness and had also washed away lingering doubts about McCloud's acceptance of their story.

After the bath, Brother Jackson took them across to the big church, then down the stairs to a small, comfortable room where a table was laden with enough steak, hotcakes, boiled potatoes, greens, apple pie and whipped cream to send Hank Brazos' easily aroused palate tingling.

"Why, you Brethren sure do yourselves proud out here in Peaceful Valley, Tucker," Brazos beamed, reaching for knife and fork. He grinned as he speared a potato. "Some eatery, eh, Yank?" He winked broadly. "How long since you ate under a church? In fact, how long's it been since you were in a church?"

"Your wit as always, leaves much to be desired," Benedict said dryly, taking a chair.

"We chose this room so thee would not be disturbed whilst thou broke thy fasts," Tucker informed them. "At other times, this is a prayer cell where the Brethren come to pray in solitude. I shall bring thee coffee, Brothers."

Tucker bowed and went out, closing the stout oaken door behind him.

Then a heavy key turned in the lock.

Deacon McCloud was addressing the special meeting of the Brethren councilors in what had once been the bar-room of the Crying Shame Saloon when Brother Tucker appeared. McCloud broke off and every man turned expectantly to the portly Tucker.

"It is done," Tucker reported, and took his chair.

"Deception is foreign to my nature," McCloud stated, "but there was no other way, without risking violence—for they are undoubtedly violent men."

"They're even worse than that," Brother Smoke said.

"That remains to be seen," McCloud said. He inclined his head at Tucker. "To acquaint you with what has transpired so far, Brother, we all seem to share the opinion that the finger of guilt points to the two men you have locked in the prayer cell. With nobody else in our valley but us Brethren and the strangers, it seems we have no alternative but to believe that they murdered our dear departed Brother. Do you also share this opinion?"

"I do," Tucker said readily, "for it is unthinkable to think that a member of the Brethren could have slain a Brother." The fat man frowned. "But, Deacon, dost thou have some doubt?"

"A just man *must* have doubt when so grave a matter is to be decided, Brother. If we pronounce these men guilty of murder, they must pay the supreme penalty; that is our way. Therefore we must be sure, and as I was just saying to our Brothers when you returned, the question that continues to confound me is ... *why*. *Why* would two such men slay a Brother? Their guns identify them as men of violence, yet they do not seem like wanton butchers. Why, not even the wolf of the forests kill without reason."

The Brethren flock nodded soberly. What the Deacon had said was indeed reasonable.

"I know a reason."

Twenty pairs of eyes went to Brother Smoke. The big man got to his feet.

"Can I speak, Deacon?"

"Any man may speak in this assembly, Brother."

Smoke's hard black eyes went from face to face before coming back to the Deacon, then his lips framed the one word: "Gold."

A murmur ran through the crowd. "Gold, Brother Smoke?" McCloud echoed. "Make yourself clear."

"I will try, Deacon," Smoke said with respect. His eyes moved from face to face as he said, "Brothers, for a long time now, we been diggin' gold here in the valley for our own use. We ain't sold any and we ain't breathed a word about the mine outside the Sourdoughs. But gold's about the loudest word in the world. Nobody can keep gold a secret forever, nobody." A deep breath swelled Smoke's chest. "It's my guess, Deacon, that these two fellers got wind of our gold and came to the valley lookin' for it."

McCloud's eyes drilled at Smoke. "Brother," he said quietly, "it could well be that you have divined a truth. Speak more. If it is as you say, that gold attracted these men, why should they murder a Brother?"

Drawing confidence from McCloud's response, Smoke continued, "I figure that when them two arrived in their boat, Deacon, they come into contact with Brother Jackson and tortured him to find out where our mine was and then they killed him. And

40

if that's the case, Deacon, they know about the mine and there's only one thing to do as I see it—unless we want the word to leak out and have our valley turned into a hell-on-wheels boom town overnight."

It was suddenly very quiet in the big room. Twenty good men and true, the Brothers were envisioning the intolerable results of a gold strike.

After a long moment, the Deacon's voice broke the silence. "What say you, Brethren? What say you to what our Brother Smoke has just said?"

At the back of the room, Brother Miller rose slowly to his feet. "I sayeth guilty."

"Guilty!" echoed the others, and the wave of sound sent the Deacon to his feet. He stretched to his full height, extended his arms and looked upward.

"Guilty," he intoned. "Guilty in the eyes of man and God." He added after a pause, "An eye for an eye." McCloud was suddenly fierce of eye and grim of jaw. And every man echoed his cry.

The Deacon raised a fist.

"A limb for a limb!" he shouted.

"A limb for a limb!" they chanted.

A throbbing pause.

"And … life for life!"

"Hanged?" Hank Brazos shouted at the voice beyond the oaken door that had told them of their fate. "You're loco, joker. What the devil are you gonna hang us for?"

"For the foul murder of Brother Jackson," said the voice of Brother Miller. "Prepare to meet thy Maker,

41

sons of Satan. Thou hast until dawn to make thy peace."

They listened to his receding steps, then Brazos crashed his great fists against the door. "Come back here, blast you! We—"

"He's gone," Benedict said calmly. "Save your breath."

Bronzed face knotted with wrath and bewilderment, Brazos dropped his fists and turned away from the door. "They're loco, Yank," he panted. "Yeah, that must be it. Every man Jack of them is tetched. They gotta be to lock us up here in the first place while they hold some kind of a trial."

"They are fanatics," Benedict said. "There is an element of the fanatic in every man who cuts himself off from the world to follow a so-called religious life."

"Well what the blue-eyed bejasus are we gonna do about it?" Brazos raged, lunging up and down the room.

Benedict shrugged in the manner of a philosopher. "What can we do?"

Brazos propped and glowered. "I don't get you, Yank. Are you fixin' to just set there on your goddamn eddicated butt and wait for 'em to haul us outa here and give us the high walk?"

"I certainly don't intend to wear myself out roaring and ranting when I know it can't do any good."

Disgust written all over his face, Brazos swung his broad back on the dandy at the table and went back to slamming his powerful shoulder against the door, even though he knew it wouldn't give.

Benedict, nowhere near as calm as his attitude indicated, took out a cigar and set it alight. As he did, the action revealed the top of the small leather holster strapped to his right wrist beneath the sleeve of his ill-fitting shirt. He traced the steel outline of the derringer with his fingers and his gray eyes turned cold. The survival instinct of a man who'd lived too much of his life in danger had prompted him to conceal the deadly little sneak when they'd handed over their Colts to Brother Tucker. The two-shot had saved his life a dozen times in the past, but never had the odds against survival been so high. Still, it was an ace to play, and even if he could not buy his life with it, he was coldly certain of one thing as he sat quietly smoking. He would take two of the Brethren into eternity with him. And one would be Deacon McCloud.

The shades of early night were falling when young Sister Susie Miller left her father's house on Charity Street. She walked to the corner and turned into Peace Street where the Deacon's house stood. Sister Susie, the prettiest unmarried woman in Peaceful Valley, had gone through a day of anguish unlike any she'd experienced in her young life, but now that she had made the decision to go to the Deacon, she felt better than at any time since she'd seen that boat washed out of Blackwater Gorge.

She found the Deacon in his upstairs study. McCloud was in somber mood, burdened by the day's events and what was to come tomorrow, but he received her with his customary courtesy.

43

"Dear Sister," he said as he held out a chair for her at the desk, "my thoughts have been much on you today. I conveyed my condolences through your father. He passed them on to you?"

"Yes, Deacon." Sister Susie's eyes showed that she'd been crying for it was only a week since she'd agreed to marry Brother Jackson. But she had not come to visit McCloud to seek comfort in her loss.

"Deacon," she said when he was seated, "is it true what my father tells me, that the two strangers are to be hanged?" McCloud nodded his big head and she said, "Then I must speak."

"Speak, my child? Of what?"

"Of their innocence. They did not murder Brother Jackson."

McCloud was out of his chair. "What is this you say, Sister? What could you know of it?"

"I … I should have spoken before, Deacon, but I was afraid, for I had broken a Brethren rule and left the settlement to meet Brother Jackson in secret." She lowered her eyes. "We had met before … by the river."

"You were at the river today?"

She looked up at him and drew a deep breath. "Yes, Deacon McCloud. I am ashamed and I expect to be punished. But at eleven this morning I went to Red Man River to meet Brother Jackson at our rendezvous by the giant sequoia. Brother Jackson was very late, but I waited, for he always came. After some time, I saw the boat run aground and watched the two strangers come ashore from concealment in the forest. For fear of revealing myself to them, I remained there until they had recovered their strength and made off towards the village. Keeping myself concealed, I followed them some distance until their dog began to bark and they came back towards me. I … I hid and waited and shortly afterwards I heard the search party arrive. I could hear all the voices, but I did not know what was happening. I waited until they had all left for town before I myself returned." Her voice caught. "It was only then that I learned what had happened to … to Brother Jackson."

"Sister, is this true? On your oath as a Sister of the Brethren?"

"Every word is true, Deacon. I swear to God on it."

Deacon McCloud let out a long breath. "You know what this means, of course? It means these men could not have slain Brother Jackson. It means that he was already dead when they arrived here."

"Yes, Deacon. And by then Brother Jackson was two hours late for our meeting. I know … I know in my heart now that he must have been dead all that time, otherwise he would have come to me."

The Deacon was stunned. The girl's confession brought forward a thought that was totally repugnant to him. If Duke Benedict and Hank Brazos had not murdered Brother Jackson, then he had been slain by somebody here in the valley. Yet, unwelcome as that idea was, it didn't dominate the Deacon's thoughts for long. The most urgent consideration now was that a great wrong had been done. It had to be made right immediately.

45

"Sister Susie," he said, placing a hand on the girl's shoulder, "because of your courage in coming to me with this truth and also in deference to your loss, there will be no punishment for your transgression. Indeed, if it were not for the fact that you broke a Brethren rule, you would not have been at the river and the terrible sin of unjust execution would have stained all of our souls forever."

"Thank you, Deacon," she said, rising. "I am grateful for—"

"We shall speak no more of it. And now, dear Sister, please go to your father and have him bring the Brethren council to the church. There is something that must be done at once."

FOUR

BLOOD ON THE DYING SUN

The derringer slipped from the spring holster into Benedict's palm beneath the table as they heard the approaching steps and then the jingling of keys.

"Step away from the door," Benedict whispered.

Brazos snorted in anger. "The hell you say. The first head that shows through there is gonna get knocked to hell and—"

Benedict showed the derringer. "I said step away from the door."

Brazos' jaw fell open in astonishment, the door swung open and Brother Tucker stood there, smiling.

"Brothers," he greeted them, and they glimpsed other black-clad men behind him. "All is understood and all is forgiven."

Benedict, his finger tight on the trigger of the hidden derringer, blinked his eyes. Hank Brazos shook his big head as if he wasn't hearing right.

"Ah, the two of thee show astonishment." The portly Tucker beamed as he waddled into the room. "And small wonder. But it is not my place to reveal the wonderful news to thee—the Deacon waits upstairs to perform that pleasant task himself. Sufficient it is for me to tell thee that thy innocence has been proven beyond all doubt. We know now that every word thou uttered was the Lord's truth."

Benedict and Brazos exchanged an astonished stare. Was this some sort of Brethren trick?

"What do you say, Yank?" Brazos asked.

The little gun was a cold weight in Benedict's hand. He stared hard at Tucker for a long moment, but the man's fraternal smile didn't falter. What the hell, he decided, sliding the derringer into the pocket of his trousers and getting to his feet—if they were playing some kind of game, he still had the deadly ace.

"Very well," he said, but the look he gave Brazos was a warning to be ready the moment treachery was shown. "We shall see what the Deacon has to say for himself."

There were more brotherly smiles when they emerged from the prayer cell, then they followed Tucker's plump figure up the steps as the others came behind. Emerging into the body of the church, they found it brightly lit with candles. A dozen more somberly garbed Brethren were seated in the front pews, turning to watch as the procession came down

48

the nave. Standing at the foot of the altar was Deacon McCloud, and at his side was the prettiest girl Duke Benedict had seen in too long a time.

The church fell silent as they stopped before the altar. Deacon McCloud smiled benignly upon them.

"Brothers, your faces are marked with bewilderment, suspicion, anger and mistrust. And rightly so, for you have been most grievously treated here this day. But, before I ask Sister Susie here to tell you what she has already told the full council, let me say, here in the sight of the Master whom we so devotedly serve, that we misjudged you sadly. It is you who are innocent, and we who are guilty and must ask your forgiveness."

Even Benedict's doubts diminished. He moved his eyes from McCloud to the girl. She blushed, then turned to McCloud and said:

"Shall I speak now, Deacon?"

"You may speak now, my child."

For a long while the only sound in the church of the Brethren was that of Sister Susie's voice—and with every word, two men who'd been facing the prospect of their last night on earth, felt the hangman's noose moving farther and farther away.

"Well, brothers?" McCloud said to Benedict and Brazos, when her story was finished. "What more is there to be said, other than that we most humbly beg and beseech your forgiveness."

Benedict and Brazos looked at each other. Then Brazos' face broke into a giant smile and the tight white lines of tension at the corners of Benedict's mouth were gone.

McCloud came forward and rested big hands on their shoulders. "Brothers, you are confounded men. But please tell us that you can find it in your heart to forgive us?"

"Perhaps," Benedict said grudgingly.

But Brazos was too relieved to hold a grudge. "Couldn't rightly blame you for jumpin' to the wrong idea about us, Deacon. And even if we never done it, you still got one of your boys done in."

"Yes," McCloud said, tight-lipped, "and we will leave no possibility unexplored until we discover who choked the life from Brother Jackson." He shook his head soberly, but then his expression softened. "For the moment, however, that grim business may be set aside. Brothers, we have committed a grave injustice against you. Now please grant us the opportunity to atone."

The full realization that the danger had actually passed hit Benedict then, and in a moment he was beginning to feel more like his poised, confident self. "I believe we can manage that, Deacon. Your wisdom in this matter gives substance to a favorite proverb of mine: The truth may be often eclipsed, but it is never extinguished."

The Brethren were suitably impressed.

Benedict, in full command now, turned to Sister Susie, gave a little bow, took her hand and lifted it to his lips. "Ma'am, I extend my thanks to you for your most timely intervention."

Sister Susie blushed and a shocked gasp went up around them. She quickly drew her hand away.

"Now what have I done?" Benedict snapped, eyes flashing.

"Do not be angry." The Deacon smiled. "We have strict regulations here. I appreciate your sentiments, but in Redemption no Brother may have physical contact with a Sister unless they are betrothed. You understand why this must be so?"

Perhaps Benedict did, but it seemed a lousy regulation to him.

Brazos said, "Sure, we understand, Deacon."

"Good, good." McCloud rubbed his big hands together. "And now, brothers, in compensation for what has taken place here today, may I ask that you permit us to extend to you both our humble hospitality. You are welcome to remain here with us as long as you wish, to rest and recuperate. What say you?"

Brazos grinned. "Why, that sounds mighty hospitable, Deacon. What do you say, Yank?"

Benedict didn't answer immediately. He was still a trifle irate over the indignities he'd suffered—and in his opinion God-fearing Redemption was just about the dullest place to spend time that he could imagine. But then, he mused, they certainly needed a rest, both men and horses. However, it wasn't until his eyes came to rest on Sister Susie that he came to a decision. Sister Susie, pretty, plump-cheeked and generously-endowed, might be in mourning, but there was in her eyes as she met his level gaze a suggestion that she might not grieve too long—particularly if she had somebody of sensitivity and consideration to help her recover from her loss. And Duke Benedict had sensitivity and consideration to burn.

"We'd be honored to accept your invitation, Deacon," he said emphatically.

"Wonderful, wonderful," McCloud said. "Members of the Brethren, show our brothers they are welcome."

The brethren responded with such enthusiasm that it took five minutes of handshakes, blessings and smiles before Benedict and Brazos emerged from the church. The street lamps were lit, the moon had risen at the end of one of Redemption's most eventful days, and the town was the picture of peace and serenity.

"Brother Samson will arrange your accommodation in the unmarried men's cottages, brothers," McCloud told them. "After you have composed yourselves, I would be honored if you would join me at supper."

"Accepted, Deacon," Benedict said. "But first, with your permission, I would like to escort Sister Susie home. She has suffered a grievous loss, and as I was the one who discovered her affianced, perhaps I might find a few words of comfort for her."

Brother Miller made to protest, but the Deacon waved him aside. "A reasonable request, and a kindly one, Brother Benedict." Then, as Benedict took the girl by the elbow to lead her down the steps, he lifted an admonitory finger. "But don't forget our regulations, brother."

Benedict dropped his hand and they strolled off, keeping a discreet distance between them.

Hank Brazos lit a badly-needed cigarette and watched them go. He had a hunch, knowing Benedict as he did, that the regulation about a man not touching a woman until they were hitched might just get a few dents put in it.

It was cool and sunny the next morning in Peaceful Valley, but some hundred miles south on the dusty plains of Arizona, where the stone and steel monster that was Placerville Penitentiary crouched on the brown banks of Crooked Creek, it was blazing hot.

From the prison farm came familiar sounds—the thud of picks biting clay, grunts from the men who wielded them—and the most hated sound of all, the dirge of their imprisonment, the clank and rattle of steel chains.

Chad Irons straightened from his toil, drawing a calloused brown forearm across his sweating forehead, his head cocked alertly. He was a tall, spare man with piercing blue eyes and a jaw that had the look of solid rock. His hands, once the most lethal in Nevada, were calloused from years of using pick and axe, but Chad Irons knew they would always be quicker with a gun than the hands of other men. He was just beginning his fourth year of a lifetime sentence for murder.

From the dappled shade of a peppercorn tree, Warder Kroner watched the tall prisoner for several seconds, then called out:

"Back to work, Irons."

The convict threw a salute. "Just as you say, Warder. Back to work."

Spitting on his hands like he enjoyed his labor, Irons swung the pick high and drove it deep into the parched soil. Beside him, the four prisoners who were his henchmen in Placerville, let their tools rise and fall without Irons' enthusiasm. Sweating profusely and cursing the flies, they worked like mechanical men, moving slowly forward, leaving a span of ripped soil behind them.

The field where the men were working was some four hundred yards outside the prison walls. Each year a detail came to dig at the parched earth and plant corn, and each year the failure of rain and the poverty of the earth saw the crops sprout feebly, wilt and die. Each spring the Warden said this season would be different, but it never was.

A canopied wagon stood in the shade of cottonwood trees on the south border of the cornfield with two unharnessed mules hobbled nearby. Between the wagon and the prison walls was a stretch of open ground clothed in dry broom sedge and rank slough grass. In that tinderbox growth, a slight wind would soon put a fire out of control.

Chad Irons' hard blue eyes drifted frequently to that field as the hot day dragged on. "Huh-huh," he would grunt in time with his thudding pick, then his gaze would move to the creek and the willows, then back to the wagon, the guards and the mules. And all the time a strange, twisted smile would tug at the corners of his wide mouth.

"Water call!"

With sighs of relief, the convicts straightened their aching backs and rested their tools against their legs. As Callaway lifted the canvas water bag off its hook in the shade under the wagon and came towards them, they took out sodden kerchiefs and swabbed at streaming faces.

Guards Larsen and Buckley stood by with rifles ready as Callaway went from man to man, filling the tin mug that hung from the water bag on a chain. Waiting patiently for each convict to finish, he wiped the cup and refilled it for the next man.

"Hot as the hobs of hell, Guard," said Chad Irons, finishing his drink and looking ruefully up at the brassy sky.

"Yeah," grunted Callaway, uncomfortable in his thick uniform.

"Sure would be nice to spend five minutes across there in the shade of them old cottonwoods. Reckon a man could work twice as hard and get twice as much done after five minutes in that deep shade."

Callaway glanced across at the trees, then back at Irons. During the two weeks he'd been working on the cornfield detail, Irons had been the best man in the party and had worked his way into the good graces of the guards.

Callaway turned to Kroner, the senior man. "What do you say?"

Kroner looked across at the jail, then ran his finger around his collar. After being in the shade, the sudden emergence into the sun had hit at him like a hammer.

"Well, they got five minutes comin'," he decided. "Ain't no regulation says they can't spend it in the shade."

"Mighty obligin' of you, Guard," Irons said to Kroner as they trooped across to the trees. "That goddamn sun would lift the skin off a lizard today."

Kroner looked at Irons curiously. He was new at the pen and couldn't figure out how Irons had got his foul reputation. As far as Kroner was concerned, Irons was a model prisoner.

Reaching the cottonwoods, the convicts seated themselves on the gnarled roots and let their hands fall at their sides, touching the dust. Kroner leaned on the wagon tongue with his rifle between his knees about five yards from the nearest prisoner, Irons. Callaway stood looking moodily at the somber bulk of the prison, his slack mouth half open and a glistening film of sweat on his face. Larsen and Buckley built cigarettes and hunkered against the wagon wheels.

Irons was the only man to stay on his feet. Whistling through his teeth he stood shuffling his boots in the dust. He seemed to be looking at nothing in particular, yet his eyes seldom left a clump of sagebrush at the base of a willow on the creek bank, where suddenly a human hand showed, waved, and vanished.

Irons went right on whistling.

A minute later he said, "Can I get another drink, Guard?"

Kroner grunted and made to get up, but Irons waved him down as he shuffled towards the wagon. "Hell no, I can get it. Stay put."

The four convicts watched Irons' every move as he stepped past Kroner. This was their moment of truth, the moment they'd waited for over the long months …

Irons didn't let them down. He whirled around suddenly and smashed his fist against the unsuspecting Kroner's jaw. Kroner went down and the convicts leaped to their feet. But Guard Larsen reacted faster than Irons had figured. As Irons lunged for Kroner's rifle, Larsen jumped on his back and shouted, "Break!" to the other guards.

Irons staggered under Larsen's weight, then thrust him off him and drove his fist into Larsen's stomach. Larsen buckled and Irons reached out for Kroner's rifle. Callaway and Buckley were diving for their weapons, but the fleet-footed convict, Pat Quill, beat them there. Then Larsen was on Irons again, grappling for the rifle. Snarling, Irons reefed the gun free and slammed the butt into the man's mouth. As Larsen staggered back, Irons raised the rifle and shot the guard between the eyes.

The shot cracked sharply in the hot air. Then Irons swung the gun around and shot Kroner who was struggling back to consciousness. Inflamed by blood lust and the smell of escape, he turned and shot the helpless Callaway in the chest. Then he swung the gun around, but Pop Harney had already accounted for the last guard with his home-made knife.

From the trees by the creek, two mounted men leading a string of saddle horses burst into view in a cloud of dust and smoke. The smoke came from the blazing wad of oil-soaked rags that Carson Bass was dragging on a length of wire. As Murch cut towards the convicts leading the horse string, Bass raced for the broom sedge strip with his firebrand.

Irons plucked the keying from Kroner's inside pocket and unlocked his chains, feeling a towering exultation. Bass and Murch, his cellmates until their release two weeks ago, hadn't let him down. The whole thing was going like a well-oiled clock.

Kicking off his shackles, Irons tossed the keys to the others and greeted big Murch with a wide grin as he rode up with the horses. As Irons swung into a saddle, the wailing howl of the Placerville siren howled across the open country. "Shake it up!" Irons shouted to the others, then he swung around in the saddle to watch Bass gallop across the broom sedge, leaving behind a red flash of blazing grass that in minutes would roar to an inferno.

The gates of the prison swung open as Pop Harney got free and Joe Pickett went to work on his chains. They could see uniformed men milling about inside the yard. Smoke was pushing their way now and they could feel the heat of the fire. "Get the fire wagon!" Irons heard a voice shout from the prison and he grinned wolfishly; they were sure going to need it.

At first the flames went straight up, then they began to lean with the breeze and the smoke grew thicker.

The last man was unlocking his chains now. Irons turned in the saddle and scowled down at the dead men. He would have liked to have rubbed out every whore's son of a guard in the whole stinking hole, but four wasn't a bad count. It was enough to guarantee that they'd never forget Chad Irons in Placerville.

Somewhere beyond the thick curtain of smoke and flame, the guards were bursting out of the gates of

58

Placerville Prison, but it was too late. With all men mounted, Irons led them at a drumming gallop for the creek. Emerging on the far side, they used their spurs and headed for the timber belt a mile distant.

Six riders stood outlined against the crimson back-wash of the hills where the sun had died minutes before. Close by a stream murmured softly against smooth stones. Away to the south, a pair of buzzards flapped away on dusty wings towards their nocturnal roost, and to the north, a thousand feet above the plains, a lone eagle soared, the sun which the men could no longer see, striking fire from its wings.

Hoof beats cut into the stillness and saddle leather creaked as they turned to see Pop Harney riding through the trees. Harney had stopped five miles back to check if they were being followed. Harney pulled his lathered horse to a halt before Chad Irons.

"Nary a sign, Chad," he reported. "They musta stayed on to fight the fire, just like you figured."

The badmen whooped at that and Chad Irons permitted himself the luxury of a smile. It was one thing to plan a crash-out, but quite another matter to pull it off so brilliantly. Thanks to careful planning and the loyalty of Carson Bass, he'd made it.

Carson Bass caught his leader's look and grinned. "Well, we made it, Chad. Straight sailin' to Peaceful Valley now, huh?"

The others looked eagerly at Chad Irons. During the long months and years, the killer had painted glowing pictures of his secret outlaw domain far away in the Sourdough Mountains of Nevada. It was the picture of a robber's roost where men could live out their violent lives untouched by the outside world of sheriffs and marshals and posse men; a law unto themselves.

"It'll be straight sailin' soon, Carson," Irons replied.

Carson Bass made to speak, but Pat Quill got in ahead of him. "Hey, Chad, you reckon there's anythin' in them rumors you've heard about a bunch o' bible-thumpers takin' over your old stampin' ground in Nevada?"

"If there is," Irons said in the hard, menacing way that was only too familiar to these men who admired and feared him, "they won't be there too long."

One-Shot Alf chuckled gleefully. To this small-time thief and bully, the idea of cleaning out a bunch of peaceful churchgoers added up to one hell of a lot of fun.

But Carson Bass wasn't grinning. "About what you said just a minute back, Chad," he said soberly. "We *are* headin' for the Sourdoughs, ain't we?"

"Sure." Irons touched his horse with steel and the sorrel jumped forward. "After I take care of one little chore …"

Nobody asked what that chore might be. When Chad Irons got that look in his eye and that note in his voice, it paid to keep quiet and go along with him. So they followed him down off the ridge and dusted north through the deepening twilight.

FIVE

SAGE JUICE AND VENGEANCE

It was springtime in Nevada and young Hank Brazos'
fancy lightly turned to thoughts of sage juice.

"Sage juice?" Benedict said.

"Hey, not too loud," Brazos warned Benedict as
two dark-garbed Brethren walked past their bench
beneath the big cedar in front of the church. "You
gotta be careful what you talk about in this man's
town, Yank."

Benedict, whose flamboyant style had seldom been
so cramped by as many rules, regulations, taboos and
restrictions as he'd been forced to cope with during
two days in Redemption, wasn't hearing anything he
didn't know already.

But he kept his voice down as he said, "What the
devil is sage juice?"

"Booze."

Benedict smiled. A picture of lazy grace in his tailored brown suit and green Prince Albert vest which Sister Susie had meticulously cleaned, repaired and pressed for him, he took out a long black stogie and set it between his teeth.

"I should have guessed." He lit his cigar. "I assume you're still feeling dry."

"Dry?" Brazos echoed, then he picked up a pebble and flicked it with deadly accuracy to bounce off Bullpup's hard head. The ugly dog, dozing in the sun, went right on snoring. "Damn it, Yank, I was dry as a powder house in Death Valley, long afore we tangled with them wagoners up north. And what have I had since? Water, coffee and even a damn mug of tea at McCloud's last night."

"Good for your soul, a little abstinence," Benedict murmured, inclining his head in the direction of the church. "The Deacon says so."

Brazos wasn't amused. "Look, Yank, I ain't no drunk. I can take hard likker or leave it be."

"But you invariably take it."

"Well, if I had my druthers, I'd druther take it than leave it."

"Which brings us back to this sage juice. Exactly what is it?"

Brazos' tone dropped to a confidential level. "It's home-made hard likker, Yank. You get yourself some cactus juice and then you add a mess of potato peelin's, and after a couple days you put in some white bread crusts. That's for the yeast, you understand? After that, you jest set back a few days until she

62

boils a bit and then if you like you can toss in a plug of tobacco for body and mebbe grind in a couple nutmegs for flavor."

The gambling man, who'd grown up with a taste for the finest wines and whiskies in his wealthy father's mansion in Boston, grimaced. "You'd drink *that*?"

"Right now I'd drink just about anythin'." Toying with the harmonica that hung from a rawhide cord around his muscular neck, Brazos looked puzzled. "You know, Yank, I don't recall ever thinkin' about booze so much in my life. Know what I reckon it is? It's all this holiness and prayin' they got goin' here … and knowin' there ain't a drop to be had in fifty miles. You get so that all you can think of doin' is somethin' you ain't supposed to."

"Perhaps. But if you're thinking of turning that foul recipe into reality—well, I'd think twice about it if I were you. Brother Thurlow tells me that the Deacon hates hard liquor almost as much as he detests adultery, murder, and whistling in church."

"I'll take my goddamn chances. Besides, she's already brewin'."

"You've made it?"

"Sure, me and old Joe Stecher. Joe was here in the old days, afore the Brethren come and they let him stay. He whomps up a jug every now and again to keep his skin from crackin' and they ain't never caught him yet. We got a big jug laid down in a cellar."

Frowning, Benedict said, "It sounds childish to me. I don't see why you can't go without liquor just for the time we're here."

"Hell, you sound just about as holy as McCloud, Benedict. Anybody'd think to listen to you that you ain't got eyes for Sister Susie. And don't tell me *that* ain't agin the regulations."

"I'm merely comforting her in her grief."

"Yeah, every chance you get. Seems to me that that little gal has got to forgettin' her dead boyfriend awful quick. As a matter of—"

Brazos broke off as a heavy dray swung into Peace Street from Hope Lane, drawn by a pair of oxen. Brother Tarr and Brother Cassidy were seated in back and Brother Smoke was driving. The two men on the bench watched in silence as the vehicle went past. Cassidy and Tarr nodded, but big Brother Smoke just stared down at them coldly, then cut at the oxen with his whip.

Benedict and Brazos wore thoughtful expressions as they watched the dray turn onto the trail that led south out of town.

"They sure got some set-up here, ain't they, Yank?" Brazos said soberly. "No sin, no troubles, best of land and water."

"Idyllic," Benedict conceded. A paradise—except for one big question mark ... the serpent in the garden ..."

Brazos nodded. "The murdered man, eh?" Benedict drew on his cigar. "You know, Reb, I've been thinking. These people have been good to us. We were in bad shape when we got here and apart from the mix-up over Brother Jackson, they've shown us splendid hospitality. I feel the least we can do for them is to try and find out who killed him."

"Couldn't agree more, Yank. But where do we start?"

"Difficult, I'll concede. The murderer had to be somebody from the valley, yet everyone here is a man or woman of the cloth, except for Stecher and a few other old-timers."

"Yeah. Well, mebbe you've raised a point there, Yank. Like you say, these folks are all mighty religious and peaceful, but they wasn't all always thataway."

"They weren't?"

"No. I been talkin' plenty to old Joe Stecher about this and he told me some mighty interestin' things about the Brethren. Seems this town was a real heller, name of Durant, afore the Brethren come, and when they took over they changed the name to Redemption and all the locals could either quit or become Brethren. Well, quite a few took to the Brethren and amongst 'em was some mighty hard characters. For instance, old Joe told me as how some of 'em have seen the inside of a jail more'n once, like Brother Gist and Brother Hursag … yeah, and Brother Smoke."

"That's interesting, Reb. Very interesting. I'd say it would be logical, seeing that we have to start somewhere, to ask a few questions about those gentlemen and keep an eye on them as well. If they're ex-jailbirds, well, despite the Deacon's theory that all men are equal in the sight of God, I still feel that leopards don't often change their spots."

Nodding in agreement, Brazos said, "What do you make of the Deacon, Yank?"

Benedict, giving the question careful consideration, got to his feet and flicked his cigar butt away. Then he started to lean on his holstered six-guns as he did many times a day before remembering that the guns were locked away in McCloud's office.

"He's a strange man," Benedict said finally. "I've spent quite a deal of time with him, but he still puzzles me. The man is as far removed from the standard idea of a preacher as it's possible to be. He is, I'm sure, totally without fear of any kind, and he seems completely self-confident. This might sound strange, but the only other men I've known with that sort of makeup were top class gunfighters."

"I hadn't figgered him that far," Brazos said, "but I sure enough got him tagged as no man to fool with."

The subject of Deacon McCloud was an absorbing one for Benedict, but suddenly he became absorbed in something else. Sister Susie Miller had just emerged from the bakery across the street. She was apparently oblivious to Benedict's presence, but he knew she'd seen him. He was also sure that she was only pretending to be examining the goods in Brother Emory's shop window.

"Well, stay lucky, Reb," Benedict grinned, and then, adjusting the angle of his hat, he set off towards the store.

"He's playin' with fire," Brazos said to his dog.

Bullpup rolled yellow eyes at Brazos and snorted to show he couldn't care less. His belly full of leftovers from the kitchen of the cookhouse that Sister Randolph operated for the unmarried Brethren, and with the warm sun on his splotched white hide, he wasn't about to start fretting about anything today. Nor was Brazos, as he got up, stretched his heavy arms and scratched his belly. There was something about the sweet air here in the high country that just seemed to sink into your bones and stop you from worrying about anything.

Except how the sage juice was coming along.

He looked about him. Benedict and Sister Susie were strolling towards the Miller house. The Deacon could be seen up on his gallery, where a few years ago the girls of the Crying Shame Saloon had danced and sung. Brother Emory was out sweeping his store porch, and over by the blacksmith's, Brothers Jefferson and Chapman were hammering a steel tire onto a buckboard wheel.

Lifting the mouth organ from under his shirt, Brazos blew a tune through it just to show everyone what an innocent young cowboy he was. Music drifting behind him, Brazos slouched off to find toothless old Joe Stecher and take a peek into the fat jug of sage juice.

The small trailside store and eatery was doing brisk business. When the customers on the southbound stage finally left, Ruck Perkins cleaned up the tables and limped into the back room to feed his pet parrot. The parrot was old and green and ate like a bald eagle. When Perkins returned to the counter he saw a man standing near the front door. He was tall and shabbily dressed. A low-crowned hat was tugged low over his forehead. Perkins put on a grin and said, "Howdy, stranger, what can I do for you?"

"I need supplies."

"You've come to the right place," the old man said, favoring his rheumaticky right leg as he walked behind the counter. "What do you need?"

"Flour, bacon, sack of salt." The tall man leaned an elbow on the counter as Perkins set about getting the goods. "Quiet, ain't it?"

Grunting as he hefted a sack of flour, the storekeeper nodded. "Now it is."

"Been here long, old man?"

Perkins swabbed at his forehead, wondering what it was that seemed vaguely familiar about his customer. "Only a couple years," he supplied.

"This work is kinda out of your line, ain't it?"

There was something about the way the man said it that bothered the storekeeper. Where had he seen that lean, hard face before?

"I was a peace officer," he said shortly. "Now, how much bacon do—"

"Why'd you quit? Get too old?"

A red flush stained ex-Sheriff Ruck Perkins' leathery features as he settled a cold stare on the tall man. He'd been a hard man in his thirty years behind a badge and he figured his two years behind a counter hadn't softened him that much. "You've got kind of a hard mouth on you, ain't you, mister?" he said challengingly.

"Wouldn't say that. Just figgered that you must have quit on account of you're old and gimpy and your memory's all shot to hell."

Perkins was growing angrier by the second. "What the devil do you know about my memory? Damnit, I—"

The storekeeper took a deep breath and threw a rein on his temper. "I'm as good a man as I ever was, if that's any business of yours, mister. Now, did you say you wanted bacon?"

"Sure," came the easy reply. "Five pounds— storekeeper."

By the time he'd cut off the slab of bacon, Perkins felt in control of himself again. He would just give the hard mouth his goods and let him get gone. "Seven-fifty all told," he said, putting the bacon on the counter beside the flour and salt.

The strange half grin was still on the man's face as he reached for the bacon. The action made the cuffs of his shirt pull back and Ruck Perkins saw the rings of white tissue encircling each brown wrist. The storekeeper stiffened. He'd seen men scarred like that before—men who'd spent time in a chain gang.

Perkins' eyes jerked up to the hard, lean face. Cold blue eyes glittered across at him and suddenly recognition hit Perkins like a punch in the stomach.

"Irons?"

Chad Irons' cruel mouth twisted. "You forgot me, old man. You forgot the day you got lucky and nabbed me at Antelope River. But you'll die rememberin' me."

Perkins' face paled. He backed off a pace. "Damn you, Irons, how did you—" He broke off and licked lips gone suddenly dry. "I … I don't even carry a gun anymore."

"I do …"

Perkins kept backing away towards the rear. But Chad Irons' right hand came over the counter with a long-barreled Colt in it. The .45 exploded and the slug hit Perkins in the middle and flung him against the cake shelves. Cakes and pies came tumbling down as another bullet ripped into his body and then he fell to the floor.

Chad Irons came around the serving shelf, smoke gushing from his gun barrel. Perkins' torso was drenched in blood. He lifted trembling hands and tried to plead, but only blood came from his mouth. "Chad Irons always settles his accounts," the killer said. He reached down with his gun until it was almost touching Perkins' face and then he pulled the trigger.

As Irons walked slowly out of the eatery two men came running his way. They stopped dead when they saw Irons' six companions ride into sight from behind the corral. Carson Bass was holding Irons' horse. He swung into the saddle and led his men towards the Sourdough Mountains.

It was six in the afternoon when Brother Smoke returned to Redemption after a hard day at the Paradise Mine. He was dirty and sweaty, but instead of heading straight for the bath-house, he guided his horse along Charity Street towards Brother Miller's cottage. He saw Sister Randolph and Sister Massey crossing Peace with flowers to put in the church, and he frowned when he caught a glimpse of a big, slouching figure in a faded purple shirt going towards the stables with a dog trailing. Smoke dismounted outside Miller's house and was hitching his horse to the fence when Miller appeared and walked down the path.

"How'd you make out?" Smoke asked.

Brother Miller, a sour teetotaler, an ascetic, and a devotee of cold baths in mid-winter, folded his arms and spoke in a quiet voice so his daughter wouldn't overhear.

"I saw the Deacon on the matter you raised with me, Brother. I informed him that you were concerned about the effect that the two strangers were having on the morality of our community, and also that I myself would prefer to see them leave."

"And?"

"I'm afraid I didn't receive a very good hearing. Not only is the Deacon bent on compensating these men for the treatment they received at our hands the other day, but I came away with the distinct impression that he is growing to like them. That is particularly noticeable in the way he talks about Duke Benedict."

"Just because he's eddicated and can spout from the Book," Smoke snarled. "Damnit, can't he see that—"

"Language, Brother, language."

Brother Smoke bit at his thick, brutal under lip. "Sorry, Brother."

Miller's gray head bowed. "No offence taken, Brother. I understand your concern over this matter, but I'm afraid that at the moment there is nothing we can do."

Grumbling goodnight, Smoke mounted up and rode for his cabin in a black mood. Reaching his destination, he saw the front door open and the lights on. He strode in to find Brothers Tarr and Cassidy waiting for him. He sailed his hat at a peg and strode to the washstand.

"How'd Miller make out, Charlie?" lantern-jawed Tarr asked eagerly.

"He didn't."

Tarr's face fell and Cassidy looked glum. It had been a tough week for Brother Charlie Smoke and his two henchmen, beginning with the near thing with Brother Jackson and now the continuing presence in town of two men who seemed to be cluttering up everything they had planned to do. Smoke had approached Miller over the attention Benedict was paying his daughter, but now that Miller's appeal to McCloud had failed, they were back where they'd started.

Charlie Smoke reflected on the situation as he sat smoking his pipe while Cassidy put on the coffee. His thoughts went back to three years ago, when the Deacon came to Peaceful Valley. In those days, Smoke had been a hard case and one of Chad Irons' minions. But then Irons, on one of his outlaw forays down south, ran out of luck and was captured by Sheriff Ruck Perkins. They'd thrown Irons into Placerville for life and that had really knocked the sawdust out of Smoke.

Without a leader, Smoke lingered on in Redemption when the Brethren took over, doing odd jobs around the town and vaguely planning to drift on one day. Then a member of the Brethren discovered gold, and Charlie Smoke came down with a dose of religion and talked his way into staying on and wearing the Brethren black. In no time at all, he was working daylight to dark at the Paradise Mine.

Smoke hadn't been too greedy or too impatient. He'd worked hard and long until McCloud and the Brethren trusted him completely; only then did he start to pilfer from the mine. That had been almost two years ago. Since then, Brother Smoke had salted away just a little over four thousand dollars in dust. It was more wealth than he'd ever dreamed of possessing.

Four thousand dollars …

The big man's gaze grew cold when he thought of the last poke he'd put in the ground. That sack of dust, which brought his cache over the four thousand mark, had spelled out death to Brother Jackson.

Soon after killing Jackson, Smoke started to think again about pulling out. With four thousand, a man could set himself up in style in a big saloon in Pueblo, or maybe in Silver City. But one big obstacle loomed.

The Deacon.

Smoke drew deep on his cigarette, his gaze on the lamp. He'd known only two men in his time who genuinely threw the fear of God into him. One was his old leader, Chad Irons, and the other was Deacon Luther McCloud. The Deacon was no thin-blooded psalm

singer like the rest of the Brethren with their sanc-
timonious thees and thous. The Deacon was a man
with a bloody background, and he could use a gun
as well as any man Smoke had ever known, maybe
even better than Chad Irons himself. And the Deacon
ruled with a hand of iron. Nobody came into Peaceful
Valley or left without the Deacon's permission. And
therein lay the rub. How did a man with a packhorse
laden down with four thousand dollars' worth of gold
get away from Peaceful Valley when the only trail in
or out was guarded day and night by the Deacon's
men? Time and time again Smoke had mulled over
the problem, but he always ended up with the same
picture in his head—the Deacon coming after him,
relentless and full of righteous wrath, and with a
hangman's rope slung over the horn of his saddle.

If Smoke was to escape, he'd have to kill the
Deacon first. A black frown cut furrows in Smoke's
brow. He had to make a final decision and make it
soon. But now, to complicate the whole damned deal,
there were these two interlopers, Duke Benedict and
Hank Brazos, who were going around asking questions and obviously trying to solve the mystery of
Brother Jackson's murder.

"I reckon we oughta sack their saddles," suggested
cruel-faced Brother Cassidy when Smoke put his
thoughts into words. "After all, we got guns stashed
away, and McCloud lifted theirs."

Tugging at his black spade beard, Smoke did some
hard thinking on that, but he didn't care much about
what he came up with. He was plenty wary of the two

newcomers, particularly Benedict. Brazos was plainly a man who would batter you into the next county with his great big fists if you gave him half a chance, but it was Benedict with his too-handsome face, his too-smooth manners and his silky way of walking that bothered Smoke most. Duke Benedict shaped up as a dangerous man in Smoke's eyes; he'd known enough of that breed to be able to make a judgment.

"I reckon we'll just play our cards close a few more days and see what breaks," Smoke finally decided. "Mebbe they'll just ride out like they say they aim to and it'll be clear sailin' again."

"Mebbe they'll go and mebbe they won't," said pessimistic Tarr. "The way they're snoopin' about askin' a whole power of questions, they seem more interested in this killin' than in leavin'."

"I said we'll wait and see, and that's what we'll damn well do," Smoke barked. "Now clear off, you two, and leave me be. I got some thinkin' to do."

The two men left. Smoke absently picked up his coffee mug, tasted it, grimaced and set it down. It was cold. He knew what he needed was a good jolt of something stronger than coffee tonight, but it wasn't to be had. Even Brother Smoke didn't dare smuggle liquor into Redemption.

Building a cigarette, the big man went onto his verandah. The moon had risen and was silvering the rooftops, throwing dark shadows of the trees across the street.

Somewhere, high in the Sourdoughs, a wolf howled. It was an eerie, lonesome sound.

Tobacco smoke trickling from his thick lips, Smoke let his eyes play over the town as he thought hard about Duke Benedict and Hank Brazos. They were the jokers in the deck he hadn't counted on. Despite the near thing with Brother Jackson, he felt his plans were going well enough, but before he made his next move, something would have to be done about them.

He considered Cassidy's suggestion again, that they try to get rid of the strangers the positive way. It had its attractions, but there were too many things stacked against it. Even if they could pull it off, a lot of awkward questions would be raised by their disappearance. No, right now that way could be too risky …

Maybe he could see Miller again. Or maybe he could figure out some way to get them discredited in McCloud's eyes and have them booted out. Possibilities ran around in his brain and made him dizzy. What he really needed was something sure and quick so he could be rid of them and get on with his ambitions.

And suddenly, just as he tossed his butt out into the street, it hit him. They were obviously men who knew the ropes; how could they resist the chance to make a lot of money—say a thousand dollars?

Excitement mounted in Charlie Smoke as he realized that with the help of the two gunnies, his problem of quitting Peaceful Valley wouldn't be a problem anymore.

SIX

THE PREACHER
WORE A GUN

The playing card nailed to the trunk of the silky oak quivered as the six-gun blasted and one red diamond spot was obliterated by a round, black-edged hole. Twice more the Peacemaker boomed and the two remaining diamonds on the number three card became bullet holes, forming a neat, diagonal pattern across the pasteboard. A fourth shot hammered the nail into the tree and the defaced card fluttered down. A final shot caught it before it hit the ground and spun it away.

As the rolling echoes of the shot drifted away from the deep gulch a mile north of Redemption, Deacon Luther McCloud walked the thirty paces to the tree. It was early morning with the sun just peeping over the rim of the gulch. The soft light glinted on the tall man's shoulder-length hair and struck a star of light from the barrel of the gun in his right hand. The

Deacon was coatless, and the early wind ruffled the full sleeves of his white silk shirt. Around his narrow, flat hips hung a gleaming black gun-rig, the cutaway holster thonged down low on his thigh.

Picking up the mutilated card, he examined it thoughtfully for a moment, then flicked it away and began to reload his gun. As he did, some instinct warned him of a presence. He whirled on high boot heels and there, framed against the rising sun on the eastern rim of the gulch, he saw a tall, still silhouette.

The way the Peacemaker leveled on the intruder's chest was an instinctive thing. The Deacon's left hand lifted to shade his eyes. When he saw who his visitor was, a tight frown creased his high forehead for a moment, then it faded and he lowered the gun.

"Good morning, Brother." His voice was polite, but there was an edge to it. The Deacon didn't like to be interrupted at his gun practice.

"Good morning, Deacon," Benedict murmured. A pause, then: "Am I intruding?"

McCloud shrugged. "Not really. I was about through anyway." The powerful features relaxed into a smile. "Come on down, Brother Benedict. Was your rest interrupted by my shooting?"

Benedict nodded as he came down the slope. A man who liked to go to bed late, and who considered any hour before eleven in the morning hardly fit to be abroad, he'd been fast asleep when the distant sounds of shooting had penetrated his cabin. Such sounds, quite common almost anywhere else, had sounded weirdly out of place in peaceful

78

Redemption, so dressing quickly, he'd made his way out to the gulch to investigate. He hadn't known just what he expected to find out here, but Deacon McCloud giving an impressive impersonation of a marksman, certainly wasn't it.

He tried to keep the curiosity out of his face as he joined the tall man by the silky oak, but he wasn't quite successful. Studying the playing card, he lifted his eyes to McCloud and saw the Deacon looking down at him with an expression that was half challenge, half amusement.

"You are perplexed, Brother Benedict. Why? Is it because you feel that weapons of destruction have no place in the hands of a man of God?"

"Something like that, I suppose, Deacon McCloud. But then, what you do or what you are is not really any of my business, is it?"

"You have the manners of a gentleman, Brother. I admire such qualities. But there is no secrecy here in Redemption. All things are clear and open in the eyes of the Lord. Ask what is on your mind. It will not offend me."

"Well, I must confess to a certain curiosity, Deacon. When you asked us to surrender our guns, I naturally assumed it was because you didn't permit any here at all."

"And that is correct. I don't allow the Brethren to go armed in Peaceful Valley, but that is to protect them from themselves. Even here, Brother, tempers do at times become frayed, and harsh words can be spoken. At such times, if men have weapons, they might use them. I merely protect my flock from themselves."

Benedict took out his cigar case. The sun had cleared the rim of the gulch now and he could feel its warmth across his shoulders. The birds that had been frightened away by the gunshots were returning to chirp in the mesquite trees along the west wall. From the direction of town came the clear sound of the church bell, calling the women of Redemption to their morning prayers.

McCloud hefted the big, black gun, spun it on his trigger finger and palmed it into the cutaway holster.

"There really is no mystery about me, Brother, once you understand what manner of man I am. You see, each man serves the Lord in his own way. Most men of the cloth preach kindness, humility, peace and brotherly love. I do too, of course, but where other pastors might only pray and hope for these things, I fight for them. I am a fighting man, not a man who cowers and prays and shields his head when Satan appears. Satan is my enemy, a fiend of power and fury, and I meet him head-on. I am ever-ready to grapple with him wherever I find him. I fight him with good deeds, with the Book, with example, but I am also ready to fight him with my sinews and my blood … or with my gun. Do you understand that, Brother?"

"I think I'm beginning to."

A big hand rested on Benedict's shoulder. "It is my way, Brother Benedict. I do not stand meekly by when I see men in sin. I seize hold of them, I shake them,

I rattle their bones. If necessary I take a whip and lash the devil out of them. If that fails, I destroy the evil altogether, even if it means destroying the man. Better a man dead than live to abuse the Lord and taint others."

Benedict was impressed by the man's fervor, but he was also a little apprehensive. For when it came to sinning, Duke Benedict could give a lot of hell-raisers a long head start. "You weren't always a preacher, were you, Deacon?"

McCloud saw Benedict looking pointedly at the gun. The big man's face shadowed. "I have been many things, Brother," and he pressed his grim lips together in a way that said the subject was closed. Then he smiled faintly. "Come, we'll return to town. You are welcome to break bread with me if you wish."

The two men were silent as they walked back through the cultivated cornfields to Redemption, Benedict reflecting on what he'd seen and heard at the gulch, the Deacon striding along with chin held high and the sunlight glinting on his hawk features. To Benedict he was the reincarnation of a fiery prophet of ancient times, a zealot striding the hot roads of Palestine and Italy, bringing with him the Word and a stout cudgel to hammer Satan into the dust.

Having already eaten with the Deacon at his residence in the converted Crying Shame Saloon, Benedict knew the preacher man enjoyed a hearty appetite, and so he wasn't surprised to sit down before a massive meal of fried ham, Johnny cakes dripping with maple syrup, hot black coffee and thick slabs of rich, home-baked bread.

McCloud was his customary, talkative self again as they took a second cup of coffee on the upstairs balcony overlooking the main street. He spoke freely and at length about his valley, his people, and the plans he had for both. Benedict was a good listener, and he was happy that the touchy subject of sinfulness had been forgotten, for back at the gulch he'd had the distinct feeling that McCloud might have been giving him an oblique warning on what was expected of him during his stay in the valley.

Then, just as Benedict was about to leave, the Deacon cleared his throat, fixed the gambling man with a stern eye and said:

"It pleases me to be able to extend my hospitality to you and Brother Brazos. With all due respect to those of my flock, I find that the pure life often robs men of a little of the strength and assertiveness of true manhood. You and Brother Brazos are undoubtedly real men … Ah, but therein lies danger, does it not, Brother Benedict?"

Instantly wary, Benedict said, "It does?"

"Indeed, and that is why I must ask you to consider carefully what I say now. Yesterday, Brother Miller came to me with a grievance. He is of the opinion that you entertain lustful feelings towards his daughter, Sister Susie. Brother Miller requested that I ask you to leave, but I decided against it. Do you know why I refused him, Brother?"

His mouth feeling decidedly dry, Benedict said, "No, Deacon. Why?"

"I told him that you are a man of intelligence and judgment, and, as such, you would not be so foolish as to incur my wrath."

Benedict looked at the man sharply. "I'll keep that in mind, Deacon."

McCloud bowed his head a little. "I can ask no more. It would grieve me to be forced to deal harshly with a man I admire."

There was no mistaking the warning in McCloud's words. Benedict's pride, always a prickly thing, was somewhat chafed.

"I hope we don't have trouble," Benedict said quietly. Then he added, "For your sake as well as mine."

McCloud's right eyebrow lifted fractionally. "A warning in reply to a warning, Brother?"

"Perhaps."

To Benedict's surprise, McCloud broke into a broad smile and clapped him on the shoulder. "Brother Benedict, you are a man with steel in him. I salute you. But on your way now if you will, Brother, for there is much that I must do. Bring Brother Brazos along to supper tonight if it is convenient. I have a great taste for the Texan's colorful stories. Go in peace."

"You, too, Deacon," Benedict said with an answering smile, and then he went looking for Brazos.

"A gunfighter?" said Hank Brazos as his eyebrows tried to meet his hairline.

83

"If he's not," Benedict said soberly, "he'll do until one comes along."

"I'll be damned." Brazos grinned and leaned back in his chair in the shade outside Sister Randolph's eatery, where he'd just polished off a double helping of steak, sourdough biscuits and grits. "You ever strike a preacher man who was a gunfighter, Yank?"

"I haven't. But then I've never struck a place quite like Peaceful Valley."

"Yeah, sure is a funny place." Brazos flipped a lump of sugar to Bullpup who consumed it with a snap of his big jaws. "And it's gettin' funnier all the time." He looked directly at Benedict. "I had a visit from Brother Smoke a spell back. He wants to see you over at his house."

"Oh? What's on *his* mind?"

"Didn't tell me. But he says it's powerful important. You reckon you'll go see him?"

Benedict frowned. On leaving the Deacon, he'd been toying with the idea of suggesting to Brazos that it might be time for them to pull out. He was in no way intimidated by what McCloud had said to him, but somewhere deep down where his conscience lived he wondered if it mightn't be better to ride out and leave these good people before he and Brazos stirred up too much dust—as they were often prone to do. The one thing holding Benedict in Redemption was the mystery of Brother Jackson's death. He wondered if Brother Smoke might throw some light on the business.

"I'll go see him," Benedict decided.

Brother Smoke was nervous as he waited for Duke Benedict to arrive. Pacing up and down his front room, he was conscious of how much depended on the success of this meeting. Then there was a rapping on the door. Smoke ground out his cigarette and opened the door to the gambling man.

"Mighty pleased you could come along, Duke." Smoke grinned and nodded towards a chair.

Benedict remained standing. "Something on your mind, Smoke?"

All business. Smoke liked that. "Dead right there is," he said, dropping into a chair and picking up his tobacco. "I got what you might call a business proposition, Duke. Interested?"

"I'm always interested in a *solid* proposition."

"Sure. You're a man of the world, just like me." Smoke licked his cigarette into shape and said, "Gold."

The cigar that Benedict was lifting to his lips came to a stop. "Gold?"

"A thousand in gold for you and your pard, Brazos. How does that hit you?"

"I suggest that you continue talking, then we shall see how it 'hits' me."

Smoke leaned forward confidentially. "Benedict, I been sizin' you up since you hit here and I got you tabbed as a feller who wouldn't turn his back on a good deal, even if there was some risk attached."

Benedict took a chair. "Please go on, Smoke."

Smoke grinned, showing big white teeth. "All right, Duke, but first I got to have your word that nothin' said here goes any further."

"You have my word as a gentleman," Benedict said after a moment's deliberation.

"Right, so I'll lay it on the line. There's gold here in Peaceful Valley. Now I don't aim to go into the ins and outs of it, but right this minute I got me a whole cache of dust—but I need a couple of good men like you and Brazos to help me get it out of the valley. For that help, I'll cut you in fifty-fifty." He made an expansive gesture. "One thousand dollars in dust."

"Have you stolen this gold?" Benedict asked.

"Does it matter how I got it? What I want to know is, are you interested?"

Duke Benedict couldn't have been a gambling man without a strong streak of avarice in his makeup. And he could use a thousand dollars. But there was a reservation. "I'm not interested in stolen gold, Smoke. Thieving is a little out of my line."

Brother Smoke talked fast then. It wasn't really like stealing, he explained. The Brethren had no use for gold other than to make their chalices and statues of worship. They took only what gold they needed. His cache was only a fraction of what lay untouched out at the mine. They wouldn't even miss it—how could that be stealing?

He talked for a long time and Benedict listened intently, feeling his reservations melting away. After all, he assured himself, it wasn't as if they were going to harm anybody just by helping ship out a small load of gold that the Brethren didn't want or perhaps wouldn't even know was missing. But uppermost in his mind was how far that thousand would take Brazos and himself in their hunt for Bo Rangle.

But in the end, when Smoke wanted an immediate answer, the caution of a man who'd often played for high stakes showed through. "I won't say yes or no, Smoke. Not yet. First I'd like to see the color of the dust."

"That makes sense," Smoke said. "Look, why don't you come out to the Paradise Mine this evenin' after we've knocked off work? I'll show you what you're shootin' for, and then maybe we can talk some more."

"Why not?"

Smoke grinned and gave Benedict directions to the mine.

"You realize I'll have to talk this over with Brazos?" Benedict said.

"Sure, Duke. Like I said, I need both of you. The only reason I sent for you alone was that I figured you got the brains and the big say."

Benedict decided then and there not to tell the Reb too much just yet. He'd wait until they had a look at the gold. He set his cigar between his teeth and studied Smoke closely.

"We may or may not have something going for us, Smoke. But one thing, friend. If this is some kind of double deal, I'd think twice about it if I were you."

The warning wasn't wasted on Brother Smoke. He'd sensed the tempered steel in the gambling man from the first. "It's a straight deal right down the line,

Duke. And I don't mind tellin' you that I need you in this set-up. Need you real bad."

"A final thought," Benedict said. "In the event that we draw cards in this game, what about the Deacon? How does he—?"

"We'll talk about the Deacon at the mine, Duke. Time aplenty then."

Benedict nodded and left. Then, passing through the gate, he paused, a thoughtful frown creasing his eyes.

How would Brazos take Smoke's proposition?

The Number Three Shaft at the Paradise Mine wasn't worked anymore and for this reason Smoke chose to meet Brazos and Benedict there. With all the workers except Cassidy and Tarr finished for the day, the old lamp lit shaft of the gold mine was as private a place as could be found in Peaceful Valley.

Smoke found himself growing tense as rendezvous time drew near. Feeling uncomfortable in the blue flannel shirt and baggy denim coveralls that he wore at the mine, he paced to and fro in the musty cavern, the bracket lamps throwing his shadow hugely on the scarred stone walls. As he walked, he was conscious of the heavy, solid weight of the gold dust sack in the right hand pocket of his coveralls. In the other pocket was the gun.

He didn't expect to use the gun, but he was prepared for the possibility. Talking over his plan with Cassidy and Tarr during the afternoon, he'd come to realize that if Benedict and Brazos rejected his offer, he couldn't let them leave Paradise Valley alive. He couldn't afford to have them go to the Deacon with the story of his offer; that would mean disaster.

He was building a smoke when footsteps echoed down the shaft and Brother Tarr came around the corner with Duke Benedict and Hank Brazos behind him.

"Well, good to see you, Brothers," he greeted, putting on a big grin, his teeth showing whitely against the black of his beard. "Okay, that'll be all, Tarr."

Tarr walked back around the bend and Smoke put a match to his cigarette. "Ever been down a mine afore, gents? I guess that—"

"We didn't come here to make small talk," Benedict said sharply.

"Why the hell *did* we come out here?" Brazos demanded of both men. The big man was in a truculent frame of mind, just as he always was when he knew Benedict was holding out on him. So far Benedict had told him only that there was a mine and they'd be having an important talk with Brother Smoke in one of the shafts. Brazos didn't like any part of it.

"Just listen and you'll find out," Benedict told him. He turned to Smoke. "Well, do we get to look at color, mister?"

"Sure enough." Smoke grinned, reached into his pocket and tugged out the small canvas sack. Smoke held the sack aloft, black eyes glittering in the lamplight.

"Here's five hundred dollars' worth of gold dust, Duke. You get the other five hundred when we're clear."

Duke Benedict's eyes shone bright. Hank Brazos' gaze flicked from Smoke to the bag, then back to Benedict. He was as suspicious as a dog in long-grass snake country. But, before he could speak, Benedict reached for the sack and said:

"Let's see what we have here."

The sack was heavy in Benedict's hands, excitingly heavy. He tugged the draw cord open and the flickering light made the yellow dust glitter. He dipped his fingers into the metal and squeezed. It was the real thing.

"All right!" Brazos said. "This here game has gone on long enough. Start talkin', Benedict."

Now that the gold was reality in his hand and not simply a word, Benedict was only too willing to talk. In his clipped eastern accents he repeated the proposition Smoke had made earlier, and went on to tell how easy it would be to leave Peaceful Valley a thousand dollars richer. It sounded good to Benedict's ears—but Hank Brazos was anything but spellbound.

"You must've got tetched by the sun, Benedict. Of all the hogswill that ever came outa a man's mouth, that wins the fur-lined bed-pot!"

"What?" Benedict was confounded by Brazos' reaction.

"You're sayin' we're gonna help this black-bearded son-of-a-bitch to steal offen all the good people of Redemption?" Brazos barked, rocky jaw out-thrust. "By God and by Judas, Benedict, I always knew as how you're a slippery varmint where a dollar's concerned, but I swear I wouldn't've believed you'd stoop this low if I didn't hear it outa your own mouth."

90

Brother Smoke's eyes became narrow slits. This wasn't going the way he'd figured. He opened his mouth to speak, but Benedict got in ahead of him.

"Now simmer down, Reb. The Brethren have no use for gold, but in case you've forgotten, we do." He held up the sack. "Five hundred here and five hundred more when we help Smoke get his cache out of the valley. Just stop and consider how far that will take us after Bo Rangle."

"The hell with Rangle! I ain't never stole a cent in my natcherl, and I'd boil in fat afore I'd take a plugged nickel offen these people and that's a fact. And what's more, mister, I'd boil in fat twice afore I'd let anybody else steal off 'em."

Benedict let out a gusty sigh. There were times when Hank Brazos was impossibly righteous and this was one of them. With the patient air of an adult explaining something to a backward child, he said:

"Reb, you're being unrealistic. Look, we're desperately in need of cash so we can continue our search for Bo Rangle. Smoke here has offered us a—"

"You look," Brazos cut him off. "I know you, Yank. Wave a dollar bill under your nose and your judgment goes for a long walk." He jabbed an accusing finger at Smoke. "You say you're willin' to pay us a thousand bucks to help get your gold outa the valley." Brazos turned to Benedict. "Okay, let's say he means it. Damn it all, man, you're supposed to be smart but it's plain you ain't asked yourself where's the catch? How come he's ready to drop a thousand bucks in our laps?"

A shadow of uncertainty passed over Benedict's face. For the past several hours all he'd been able to think about was the thousand in gold and how badly it was needed. But Brazos, in his bull-headed way, for once seemed to be dealing in logic.

"Yes," Benedict conceded grudgingly, "I suppose it is a great deal of money." Benedict looked directly at Smoke. *Is* there a 'catch'?"

Smoke swallowed. Things were slipping away from him. But he was in too deep now. He had to keep on, there was no going back. His grin was painful as he said, "There ain't no catch, Duke. The deal is just like I say. You help me get the gold out and—"

"Why do you need our help?" Brazos asked.

"It's the Deacon," Benedict said. His brain was working clearly now and his normally suspicious nature was again asserting itself. "That's it, isn't it, Smoke? You're expecting trouble from the Deacon and you need our help in handling him. You're afraid of the Deacon, aren't you?"

There was a moment's silence, then Smoke's face twisted in anger. "McCloud is a lunatic!" he raged. "He killed so many men when he was a gunslinger that it scrambled his brain."

"You want us to kill the Deacon," Benedict said quietly. His lips curled in contempt. "Well, mister, I fear you have misjudged us badly. Perhaps, as my partner says, I do have a weakness for a dollar, but I am no killer."

"You—you just don't understand the situation," Smoke muttered.

92

"We understand all the way," Brazos said. "We know your dirty breed backwards."

Something flashed across Smoke's eyeballs. "Then there's no deal?"

"You catch on real quick," Brazos said.

Brother Smoke's heavy shoulders sagged at that. Shaking his head, he made as if to slip the gold sack back in the pocket of his coveralls. But the sack dropped, then his hand plunged into the pocket and lamplight glittered on the gun that came out. Smoke turned the gun on Brazos … and froze, gaping at the thing in Duke Benedict's right hand.

"I was less than truthful with the Deacon when he insisted we turn in our guns," Benedict said with a cold smile, as he slowly raised the wicked black muzzle of the sneak gun until it was trained squarely on the gaping Smoke's forehead. "But a gambling man without a sneak gun is a gambling man who won't see the age of thirty. All right, Reb, get that hogleg."

Indecision worked across Smoke's features as Brazos stepped towards him. He brought the gun up an inch, hesitated and started to lift it again, but by then it was too late. Brazos' big hand wrapped around the barrel of the gun and the other hand became a ham of a fist that smashed into the side of Smoke's jaw, knocking him to the ground.

"If there's one thing I can't abide, it's ugly varmints throwin' down on me," Brazos growled. He thrust the six-gun into his belt and reefed the big man to his feet. "Just can't abide it," he repeated, and then he slammed his fist again into Smoke's face.

Smoke was a big, powerful man, but he'd never been hit this hard in his life. Blood running from his nose and mouth, he crashed against the wall of the shaft, shook his head to clear it, then, mouthing a bloody curse, he swung a looping right at Brazos' head.

The punch missed and Brazos drove his fist into Smoke's belly. The man jack-knifed, eyes popping. His mouth sucking for air, he collapsed to the ground, his hands clutching his belly.

Brazos hauled the six-gun from his belt and Benedict swung his derringer at the sound of running boots. Cassidy and Tarr swung around the corner and skidded to a stop.

"Vamoose!" Brazos barked.

"Fast!" said Benedict.

Smoke's men weren't about to argue, not when Charlie Smoke was kissing dirt and two guns were pointed their way.

They about-faced and fled.

"All right, let's hear from Brother Smoke," Benedict said.

A groan escaped from Smoke's lips as Brazos twisted a hand into his shirt and hauled him to his feet. Brazos slapped him hard on one side of the face, then the other. Sweat and blood flew. Brazos drew his right hand back again, but hesitated. He looked a question at Benedict, who frowned and then shook his head.

"He's had enough."

94

Brazos released his grip and Smoke slid down the wall until he was squatting on his boots. He looked like he'd fallen from a fast train.

"Mebbe you're right, Yank," Brazos growled. "Anyhow, I reckon he'll get more of what's comin' to him when the Deacon finds out what's been goin' on."

Smoke's eyes got big. "You—you ain't tellin' the Deacon?" he said hoarsely, trying to rise. "You—listen, you can't do that."

Brazos grinned. "Sure looks like we hit a raw nerve, Yank."

"It may be more than just fear of the Deacon," Benedict said thoughtfully.

"Whaddya mean?"

"Look at him, Reb. Take note of the sweat on his face. It's cool in this shaft."

Smoke's tongue flicked out. "The Deacon—he'll kill me."

"Just for stealing gold?" Benedict said.

"You don't know him—he's crazy, I tell you!"

"The Deacon's a fair-minded man," Brazos said. "He'll think of a fittin' punishment."

Smoke's chin trembled. "You two don't know him like I do."

"Reb," Benedict said, "he may be right."

Brazos looked at his trail partner in surprise. "You think the Deacon would—"

"Let's stroll down a way so we can talk in private," Benedict said, grasping Brazos' arm. When they were well out of earshot Brazos said:

"I reckon we just gotta tell McCloud. He's got a right to know about this thievin' varmint."

"He does have the right," Benedict agreed. "However, we must think of ourselves."

Brazos' forehead grew furrows. "Whaddya mean by that?"

"Well, Reb, the good Deacon is so tied up in knots about righteousness and sin that he's not what I would judge to be a normal, rational man. What if he doesn't believe our story?"

"Why shouldn't he? We ain't liars."

"Perhaps he feels that Brother Smoke isn't a liar. After all, what proof against Smoke do we have to offer?"

"There's the bag of gold dust."

"There is no way to prove that Smoke stole that dust. Smoke could say it belongs to us. He could also say that we made up the story for reasons of our own."

"What kind of reasons?"

"Brother Smoke would think of some. His brain is probably spinning in that direction at this very moment."

The furrows in Brazos' forehead grew deeper. "You're sayin' that the Deacon might believe Smoke and then turn on us, eh?"

"It's a definite possibility. If he thought we were lying to discredit a member of the Brethren—yes, he could well turn on us."

Brazos spat in disgust. "I sure as hell hate to let that varmint go free as a jaybird."

"So do I. Now think of this, Reb. Men have killed for gold before today and they'll continue to do so until the world spins off its axis."

"What's that got to do with—" Brazos cut himself short. "Gold. Brother Jackson."

Benedict smiled. "Exactly."

"You think Smoke killed Jackson?"

"It's a possibility we could explore."

Brazos nodded. "Provin' who killed Jackson—that'd be one way to pay back the Deacon for how good we've been treated."

"A superlative way," Benedict said, and at the same time he was thinking that some of the gold from the Paradise Mine could find its way into his saddlebags.

"What'll we do about Smoke right now?" Brazos asked.

"We'll let him go. That of course will seem strange to Smoke, so we'll tell him that it suits us at present to keep Deacon McCloud from erupting into the wrath of righteous indignation."

Brazos blinked at the big words. "You better tell him."

"He probably won't accept it," Benedict said.

"That I don't doubt."

"Which will be just fine."

"Huh?"

Benedict smiled almost paternally at his uneducated trail partner. "A man who is worried and puzzled, Reb, is a man likely to make a mistake. Come. We'll give Smoke a boot in the pants to freedom, then we'll return to town. The Deacon expects us for supper."

SEVEN

OUTLAW'S
SHADOW

"Duke, I thought you stopped by to ask me some questions about Brother Smoke," Susie Miller said.

"And so I did, Susie," Benedict murmured as his lips brushed her small, shell-pink ear. "But that was before I saw you by lamplight in that classically beautiful gown, and—"

"It's not a gown, it's a nightdress."

"It is?" Benedict tried to sound surprised. His eyes went over the girl's bare shoulders, then the soft, creamy curve of her breasts. "Well, I'll be ... so it is."

Pretty Sister Susie blushed and smiled, but she couldn't conceal her apprehension.

"Duke," she protested, acutely aware how handsome he looked beside her on the sofa with his gray eyes half closed, "if father should come in—"

"Your father, bless his God-fearing soul, is visiting the Deacon," Benedict told her. In fact, Brothers Miller and Tucker had called on McCloud while he and Brazos were drinking after-dinner coffee with the Deacon. Benedict, a born opportunist, had decided that this was the perfect time to stop by at the Miller house.

"He could come back any minute," she said, running a finger down his cheek.

"He's talking to the Deacon about the corn crop," Benedict murmured, taking her into his arms and meeting no resistance at all. "Serious business, corn crops, Susie. They could be occupied for hours ..."

Sister Susie, happy to be convinced, suddenly threw aside what little restraint she had left and drew Benedict to her with fierce, hungry urgency, then crushed her sweet red lips against his.

Being only human and a thorough gentleman, Benedict responded, and he was still responding in fine style a minute later when the door opened and Brother Miller strode in.

Time, as they say, seemed to stand still. Then Sister Susie, flushed, disheveled and wide-eyed, jumped to her feet in total confusion. She tried to fix her hair and gown at the same time while Benedict, no stranger to awkward situations such as this, got to his feet gracefully and gave Susie's stone-faced father what he hoped was a winning smile.

"Ah, Brother Miller! Through already, eh? I just stopped by to return a book your daughter kindly lent me. Well, now, Brother, how did the corn crop discussion—"

"Lecher!"

"Pardon?"

"Seducer!" Brother Miller accused, trembling head to foot. "I have suspected from the start that you had lustful designs on my daughter—and now I've caught you in the act." His voice rose. "Servant of the Devil! Carnal monster!"

It was distressingly plain to Benedict that it was time to go. Smiling apologetically at Susie, he picked up his hat. But Brother Miller barred his way.

"You will know the wrath of the Deacon for this black deed, Brother."

"I hope not," Benedict said. "But there is one thing I *do* know, Brother."

"What, curse you?"

"I, sir, know my Redeemer liveth."

Miller gaped. "He—He does live!"

"Indeed He does," Benedict assured him, and then, taking advantage of Miller's momentary confusion, he stepped lightly past him and was gone.

It was like old times, almost as if Chad Irons hadn't been missing for nearly four years. The tall killer was standing at his old place at the long bar of Wainright's Trail End Saloon with a glass of whisky in his fist, a gun on his hip, and an aura of explosive violence that surrounded him like heat coming off a flat iron. The barflies, cowboys, towners and loafers knew all about the bloody breakout from Placerville and were impressed with the bunch of hard cases the wild man had brought back with him. But even if Irons had returned unheralded and alone, he would still have commanded the same awed respect as he'd been afforded in his three hours in town.

Though it didn't show in his gaunt, hard face, Irons was enjoying the sensation his return had caused, and he was listening poker-faced to barkeep Pinky Grant tell him how great it was to see him out, fit and free again, when Carson Bass shouldered through the batwings and crossed to the bar.

"Hey, Chad," Bass grinned, jerking his thumb over his shoulder. "I just seen one of 'em."

"One of who?" Irons' tone was lazy.

"One of them Brethren jaspers they been tellin' us about. Just seen him goin' into the store."

Irons' glass hit the bar with a thump. He didn't look lazy now as he straightened, hitching at his belt. The rumors he'd heard about a bunch of religious cranks taking over his valley fifty miles north in the Sourdoughs had been confirmed by the towners of Wainright. "The store you say?" he said quietly, and when Bass nodded he tipped his battered hat forward and strolled towards the batwings. An expectant look passed amongst the other former inmates of Placerville; scenting a little excitement, they set their drinks aside and followed him out.

The badmen came to a halt on the edge of the gallery. Wainright's rutted, crooked main street was a rusty red snake winding through a miserable collection of frame houses, lean-to saloons and a grotesque, angling hotel. A saddle horse and pack mule stood racked out front of the general store opposite the Trail End. Irons stood with hands hooked in his shell belt, watching the gloomy square of doorway. Presently a man came out humping a sack of flour. He was tall and skinny and was dressed in an ankle-length black robe. He loaded the sack, then went back inside, and when he came out again toting a big wooden crate of canned goods, seven men were standing in the hot sun by the hitch rack.

Brother Wilson propped a moment in surprise, then put on a toothy grin.

"Morning, Brothers," he greeted them.

"Why, mornin' to you, too," Chad Irons said amiably, stepping forward. "Would you be the leader of the Brethren we hear about up in Durant, Brother?"

"Oh heavens, no," Wilson said modestly. "Our leader is Deacon McCloud, and the name of our town is now Redemption."

Chad Irons took a backward step. For one moment there was naked murder in his eyes—and then the terrible look was replaced by a smile. "Help you with that crate, Brother?"

"Why, I thank thee, Brother," Wilson said. "But I think I can manage."

"But I insist." Irons stepped forward, took the box from Wilson's arms and inclined his head at the mule. "You want it lashed on that there pack-mule?"

"Indeed I do, Brother." Wilson beamed, not seeing the sly, expectant grins on the faces of the others. "And the Lord's blessing be upon you for your kindness."

"Not at all," Irons replied, and turning, made as if to heave the crate onto the back of the mule, but he sent the box over the animal's back. There was a crash, and cans of peaches, beans and lard burst free and went rolling across the street.

"Damnation," Irons said, shaking his head. "Ain't I the clumsy one?"

Trusting Brother Wilson still didn't realize what was going on until One-Shot Alf cackled. The man's face reddened then as he turned to see a row of grinning faces. Only then did he become aware of the other men watching with vast amusement from the gallery of the saloon.

Wilson looked pleadingly at Irons, but he found no comfort there. He hesitated, then started to walk around the mule to retrieve his cans. But a boot was thrust between his legs and he went sprawling.

"Now that ain't no way to treat a man of the cloth, boys," Chad Irons chided. "Help him to his feet."

Ready hands reached down for the half-stunned Wilson. He was jerked to his feet, and they started batting him between them, forming a circle and thrusting him from one to the other. Wilson tried to protest but the rough laughter drowned him out. His cassock was coated in dust and his face was burning red. The shoving grew to be more like blows now, and he grunted each time a pair of hands made contact. Twice he fell and twice they reefed him up and started buffeting and rolling him around the derisive circle again. He wanted to cry out for help, but he knew there was no one to help him here. And then, just as he feared he might lose consciousness, the tall man with the hawk face pushed his way through to him and ordered the others to stop.

"Goddamn it all, boys," Chad Irons remonstrated, putting a supporting hand around the unsteady black-garbed figure, "you always go too far." Then he turned to Wilson. "You'll have to forgive my lads, Brother, but we're just in from the wilds and they're full of sass and vinegar. This is only their way of havin' fun, but I can see plain as day you ain't enjoyin' it." He waved a hand. "Come on, boys, make way. The Brother needs a little water to cool him down."

In full possession of his faculties, Wilson might have detected the heavy irony in Irons' voice and seen the wicked gleam in his blue eyes as he made an elaborate show of leading him to the horse trough nearby. But Wilson, dazed and bewildered, thought Irons was helping him and he muttered profuse thanks.

"Not at all, Brother," Irons assured him. "Come on, you just douse your head in there and you'll feel like a new man in jig time."

The cool water was like a benediction as it closed over the bending Wilson's burning face. His hands gripped the sides of the trough and he kept his face immersed for a full delicious ten seconds, but then, as he made to lift his dripping head, a powerful hand came down on his skinny neck and thrust his face under again.

Wilson struggled frantically but Irons kept his face pressed against the slimy bottom of the trough. He sucked in water through his nose and mouth, the world turned dark and his lungs felt like they were bursting. Then another great gush of water burst past his lips, his senses reeled and blackness hit him like a club.

Wilson's first awareness of returning consciousness was the feel of something pressing against his face. He thought it was the bottom of the trough and he cried out in terror. Then, jerking upright, he found he was seated on his horse.

Slowly the false-fronts stopped swirling and the scene came into focus. He saw the buildings clearly, the hot sun, the gaping faces of the onlookers. And encircling him, the faces of his tormentors.

The man's bulging, water-reddened eyes came to focus on the tall man holding his horse's head. "Why, Brother?" he panted, water dribbling from his mouth. "Why didst thou misuse me in—"

"Don't brother me, you milksop bastard," came the harsh reply from Irons. "The name is Irons. Chad Irons."

The way Wilson's sorry face sagged showed he knew the name. A powerful hand reached up and squeezed his arm.

"Yeah, you've heard of me all right, mister. And I've heard of you and that bunch of holy rollers camped up there in my valley. Now the only reason I'm leavin' you go alive, mister, is so you can get the hell up there to Peaceful Valley and tell McCloud he's got forty-eight hours to vamoose—lock, stock and barrel because I'm comin' in. You get that, Brother? If you

ain't all gone in forty-eight hours, you ain't never
gonna leave there at all."

Wilson nodded weakly and then a powerful slap sent
his horse lunging away. Chad Irons spat in the dust.
Then, in case any of them had any doubts about how he
felt about the current occupants of his hidden valley, he
said, "Nobody takes nothin' off Chad Irons. Nobody!"

The face of Deacon McCloud looked more saddened
than angry in the light of his study lamp as he stared
across the desk at an indignant Brother Miller.

"What you tell me is true, Brother Miller. There is
no exaggeration?"

"None," Miller assured him, wearing the look of a
man ready to break out the tar and feathers. "I caught
them enmeshed in their lust in my very parlor … a
terrible sight for a man to see, Deacon, terrible."

McCloud sighed, his fingers moving across the
leather binding of the Bible in his hands.

"Regrettable, Brother, most regrettable …"

"Regrettable?" Miller echoed. "Is that all you have
to say, Deacon? You, who hate the world of the flesh
as much as I? Upon my soul, I expected that the
moment I conveyed this evil news to you, you would
be seeking out this lecherous interloper and—"

"Do not excite yourself, Brother," McCloud interrupted. "He will be punished."

Miller brightened. "The lash?"

McCloud shook his big head, his long black hair making a rustling sound against the collar of his frock coat.

"Brother Benedict is not one of us, Brother Miller. If he were, I would certainly order the lash. But he is an outsider, not bound by our rules. He and his partner will be told to go."

Brother Miller's face turned ugly. "So ... so I can see it is true, Deacon."

"What is true?"

"What some of the Brothers have been saying, that you have developed a friendship for these interlopers—even though it was plain from the moment they came here that they were troublemakers and scoffers at our way of life."

McCloud's chin lifted. "I shall not deny that, Brother Miller. My hand of friendship is out to any man, sinner or saint. Have you forgotten the story of the shepherd and the lost lamb, Brother?"

"No, I haven't forgotten, Deacon McCloud. But I think you have forgotten the precepts of our beliefs and have—"

McCloud's big hand hit the desk with a hard slap. "Enough, Brother Miller. I do not propose to be censured by you or any man. I have listened to your complaint and I've made a decision. You will abide by it without further argument."

The anger in Miller's face disappeared in an instant. Cowed by McCloud's force of personality, he bowed his head. "As you say, Deacon McCloud."

Impatience clouded McCloud's eyes. "Leave me now. Find Brothers Benedict and Brazos and send them to me."

Miller left without another word. Banishment might not be as satisfying for an outraged father as fifty lashes, but at least the gambler and his uncouth friend would be gone and his daughter would once again tread the paths of righteousness.

He went to the cabins that Benedict and Brazos occupied on Charity Street, but the men weren't there. Somebody told him that the two outsiders had gone towards old Joe Stecher's shack some twenty minutes earlier.

Miller headed for Stecher's, relishing what was to come, when the sound of hoof beats drifted in from the river trail. Then Brother Wilson rode in with Chad Irons' ultimatum that jolted everything else, Benedict included, from Brother Miller's head.

"Who's Chad Irons?" Hank Brazos asked in puzzlement when an uproar brought him and Benedict out of old Joe Stecher's shack and they heard half the population of Redemption murmuring the outlaw's name.

"You mean you ain't never heard of him?" asked diminutive but sprightly old Stecher.

"Obviously everybody else here has," said Benedict, frowning at the alarmed faces of the men and women gathered before the church.

"Sure they have," said Stecher. "This was Chad Irons' town once."

"So who the hell is he?" Brazos demanded impatiently.

Stecher's wrinkled face went vinegar sour. "Chad Irons is just about the meanest varmint west of the

Mississippi. You could call him a gunfighter, a rustler, an outlaw and a whole mess of other nasty things and you'd be right. Like I say, Redemption used to be Chad's town a few years back, but it was called Durant then. She was an outlaw town then—no law at all except what Irons decided. 'Twas only when he left here to rob a bank that a lawman spotted him down south and got him throwed into jail for life on an old murder charge."

"You sound like you knew this Irons feller personal," Brazos said.

Stecher nodded. "I sure did. If you recall, I told you I was here afore the Brethren came. I wasn't no badman though—just the blacksmith, like now. But I knew Irons right enough."

Stecher broke off, looking upward. Following his stare, Benedict and Brazos saw that the Deacon had appeared on his balcony across the street. The crowd fell silent as McCloud lifted his hands. Even at that distance they could see how grim he looked, the night wind blowing a lock of black hair across his forehead.

"Brothers and Sisters, return to your homes," the Deacon said. "You have, I know, heard the evil news of the avowed return of Chad Irons and his wicked breed—an event we did not anticipate might occur. However, go home, pray, and above all have no fear. The situation is well in hand. Your Deacon will see to it that no harm befalls you."

Reassured by McCloud's calm words, the crowd began to slowly disperse. Through the open French doors leading to the Deacon's study, Brazos and

Benedict caught a glimpse of Miller, Smoke, Tucker and several other sober-faced members of the Brethren.

"You got to hand it to the Deacon," Stecher said admiringly.

They thought the old man was referring to how McCloud had handled the crowd, but Stecher's next words told them otherwise:

"Yes, sir, only the Deacon could stay that calm and collected with a geezer like Irons comin' after his scalp."

Two pairs of eyes swung on the old man. "You say Irons is comin' for the Deacon?" Brazos said. "What the hell for?"

"Hell, you don't know anythin', do you, son?"

"How could we? Nobody's told us nothin' … leastways nothin' about this Irons business. Come on, spill it out, Joe. What's the story?"

"It goes way back," the old man said. "In the old days the Deacon and his kid brother were hell-raisin' gunfighters known all over Colorado. The Deacon had claimed some of the biggest gunfighter scalps in the West. Then Chad Irons killed the Deacon's kid brother and the Deacon went huntin' him."

"So that's his stamp," Benedict said soberly.

"One of the best, he was," Stecher went on. "Fact is, a lot said he was the *very* best until he set his guns aside and took to the Lord's work full-time."

The old man's story explained a lot of things that had puzzled Benedict and Brazos in Peaceful Valley.

Lighting a long, black cigar, Benedict murmured, "Keep going, Joe."

"Well, the Deacon went searchin' for Chad all over. Took him a long time but he finally came to the Valley—only to find that Irons had been nabbed by the law and was rottin' in Placerville for life." He spread his hands. "The Deacon felt guilty about his kid brother gettin' killed. It was on account of that that he quit gunslingin' to take up religion. He got to takin' a good look around here and decided this was the place the Lord meant him to bring his people to. Well, he done it, kicked all the no-goods out and built his church. I reckon he figured he was set here for life ... but it don't look that way now."

It was an incredible story, but they'd been aware all along that the Deacon was a rather incredible man. They would have liked to have heard more from Stecher, but Brazos decided they should go straight up and see McCloud.

"Do you think that's such a great idea?" Benedict queried. He hadn't told Brazos what had happened at Miller's house earlier. If Miller had gone to see McCloud, then Duke Benedict's popularity with the Deacon would be around zero right then.

"The man's got a problem, ain't he?" Brazos said. "Mebbe we can help him out some."

Benedict, never nearly as anxious as his trail partner to leap to the aid of the unfortunate, nevertheless agreed, though for what reason he wasn't quite sure. Even if Miller had reported that innocent little encounter with Sister Susie, Benedict reasoned, the Deacon would have too much on his mind tonight to be concerned with trivia of that sort.

111

Leaving Stecher, they crossed the street to the Deacon's house, but as they reached the doors they encountered Miller and the others coming out. The Deacon was not to be disturbed, they were told. He had locked himself away upstairs with his Bible and was praying to the Lord for guidance in what Brother Tucker, quoting the Deacon's own words, described as "Redemption's darkest hour."

EIGHT

FACE THE GUN

The midnight wind stirred the willow fronds along the quiet, sandy bend of Red Man River fifteen miles downstream from Peaceful Valley. The shadows shortened as the brilliant yellow moon approached its zenith. On the sandbanks, a fat gray badger sat as still as a stone. And then, from beyond the bend where the sycamores grew close, came the sound of hoof beats and the badger scuttled for cover.

The riders emerged from the trees and rode into the clearing by a deep pool. There were seven of them; hard-faced, silent men who reined in when Chad Irons held up his hand. He stepped down.

"We'll spell here." Irons' voice was harsh, rough-edged.

The name McCloud had plainly jolted Chad Irons in Wainright, but even after the long, forced ride along the little-used river trail had brought them

113

thirty-five miles north of the cow town, Irons' men were still in the dark about McCloud. Irons had been tight-mouthed and silent throughout the ride; but now, as they off-saddled and set about brewing coffee to counteract the night's chill, Carson Bass decided it was time to clear the air. If there was trouble brewing, he told Irons, he reckoned they had a right to know what it was all about.

This attitude could have earned Bass a snarling retort or a backhander to the mouth, but it didn't. Irons, sprawled out on the sand with a mug of whisky-strengthened coffee in his hand, felt he was ready to let his men in on the mystery.

Clustered around the leader with cigarettes and coffee, the six ex-cons listened in silence as Irons related the story of his clash with the youthful gunslinger, Darcy McCloud, in Colorado Territory. He'd slain McCloud and had been wounded himself, but only after the killing did he learn the name of the man he'd gunned down. Soon after that he discovered that Darcy was the brother of a lightning-fast gunslinger known as Luther McCloud.

The respectful way he spoke of the elder McCloud brought looks of surprise to the faces of men who were familiar with Irons' lack of esteem for any gunfighter. Irons saw the looks and was moved to explain.

"McCloud would have been the best gunslinger in Colorado at the time," he said, then added quickly, "outside me, of course. I saw him tangle with three good men in Clanton City a couple years afore and he triggered 'em down like ducks. In his day he rubbed out jaspers like Fast Tom Hendry, Wyoming Terrill and Joe Burns." Irons shook his head. "Fast he was, real fast, even if he was well past forty then."

"What happened after you plugged his brother, Chad?" Pat Quill wanted to know.

Irons' cruel face darkened. "He come after me." The killer's mouth twisted as if he were tasting something sour. "Anybody else, I'd have let him catch up with me and blown him to kingdom come. But I'd stopped lead in my gun arm against his kid brother and that was a shade of odds you couldn't give a gunman like McCloud." He sucked in a deep breath. "So I ran. I ran all the way back to Peaceful Valley. After that I heard no more of McCloud. I mended, then I kept on livin' like always … until the day Ruck Perkins nabbed me and I went to prison."

The badmen were impressed, both by Irons' honesty in admitting he'd fled, and in the picture he painted of Luther McCloud.

"Why do you figure McCloud came to the Valley in the first place, Chad?" Pop Harney asked after a silence.

Broad shoulders shrugging, Chad Irons replied, "Who knows? But my guess is that McCloud finally dogged me to the Valley, then elected to stay on."

"But you don't mean for him to stay there much longer, eh, Chad?" Carson Bass said with a broad grin.

Moonlight glinting on the six-gun sagging from the cutaway holster on his hip, Chad Irons uncoiled to his feet and tossed his coffee dregs into the pool.

115

"He's took what's mine," he said in a voice that sent a thrill through his listeners. "Nobody does that to Chad Irons." His right hand blurred and his gun streaked into his hand. It was an incredible draw honed to perfection by years of daily practice with a carved replica of a six-gun in Cell 389 in Placerville Penitentiary. "And I ain't carryin' no lame arm now. I beat his brother and I'll beat him."

There were no more questions to ask. Irons had said it all.

"We know the whole story, Deacon," Benedict said to McCloud in the latter's study.

"Includin' how this Irons killed your brother," Brazos said, "and how you was once a gunslinger."

"And you're shocked?" the Deacon queried. "Well that is understandable. I killed nine men in my time. Some deserved it, but others I could have let live. I'm not really proud of my past, but there is no changing it. The one thing I deeply regret is that I feel I led my brother astray, that I was responsible for his death at Irons' hands.

"Yes, I suppose you were shocked," McCloud went on when neither man spoke. "But such a thing is not so strange. A man can take many a wrong turning in life before he finds the right path. I have no regrets for what I once was—I am simply grateful that I was shown how to come out of the darkness into the light."

"What you once *were*, Deacon?" challenged Benedict, seated with long legs crossed, across the

116

desk, a long cigarillo in his hand. "You are still a man of the gun."

"Of course, but now my gun is used in the Lord's service," McCloud replied without hesitation. He leaned over his desk. "Now, Brothers, let us get down to business. I regret that I had to keep you waiting so long to see me tonight, but I had to seek the Lord's guidance in this … this dark matter that has thrown a cloud over our Valley. Why have you come to see me?"

Hank Brazos glanced at Benedict, then said, "Well, I don't know about the Yank here, Deacon, but I reckon I've come to say as how I'd admire to lend you a hand if you look like runnin' into trouble with this Irons feller."

The Deacon's grim, hard face softened at that, and a warmth came into his eyes. "Why … why, that is a noble sentiment, Brother Brazos, a most generous thought." He shook his head wonderingly. "Who knows but that the Lord may have directed you here in our hour of need. Strange are the ways of the Lord. Do you share our Brother's sentiments, Duke?"

Benedict studied the burning tip of his cigar. He was reflecting on all the terrible things that could happen to a man who decided to play hero. Yet, somehow, despite himself, it seemed, when he looked up to meet McCloud's gaze, he found himself shrugging indifferently and saying, "I believe I do, Deacon."

"Spoken like a man, Yank." Brazos grinned. "Well, what do you say, Deacon?"

117

A broad smile illuminated Deacon McCloud's face as he got to his feet. "What can I say but … thank you, Brothers. I am, of course, completely confident that, with the Lord watching over our cause, we shall triumph over these running dogs of Satan, but I must also concede that what with my followers being mostly men of peace, your support will immeasurably strengthen our sinews of war."

A lot of the words were too big for Brazos, but he got the drift. "Okay, Deacon, then it's decided. But we'll need our guns."

"Of course. See Brother Tucker. He will return your weapons to you. You are of course free to handle whatever may befall in any way you wish, but if you choose to accept direction from me, then I would be obliged if you would ride out to Bear Trap Pass where I have posted four Brethren to keep watch. You could make certain that all is in order, then report back to me."

"Good as done," Brazos said, and headed for the door.

"One last thing," McCloud said, coming around his desk. "I feel I must be completely honest with you at this moment, and what I have to say concerns you, Brother Benedict."

"Sister Susie?" Benedict hazarded.

"Unfortunately, yes. I do feel that Brother Miller tends to exaggerate things, Brother, but our rules must be kept, so I regret the necessity of saying that when this matter of Chad Irons has been resolved, I shall have to ask you to leave our Valley."

"What about Sister Susie?" Brazos asked. "What happened?"

"It was nothing of consequence," Benedict said. He gave McCloud a little bow. "I understand, Deacon. Perhaps it will be for the best. It's time we were moving on anyway."

"Good. There is no barrier between us now." McCloud put a big hand on each man's shoulder. "Then we shall gird our loins and fight Satan together, Brothers."

NINE

SWEEP OF FURY

Deep in the brush that crowded the flanks of the river pass a hundred yards from where Hank Brazos stood watch, something moved. Brazos, crouched low in a niche of rocks with his Winchester in his big hands, went still as stone, his blue eyes probing the dappled shadows. He and Benedict had been on guard at the pass for the past twelve hours, and Benedict had left thirty minutes ago to report back to the Deacon that all was quiet.

But *was* it quiet?

He couldn't see anything down there, but danger-honed senses kept his neck hair bristling. It was too quiet along Red Man River, and that stir of movement didn't tie in with any bird or animal he could bring to mind.

A moment later he let the hiss of a held breath go. He'd caught the brief flash of sunlight on steel, and now he glimpsed the dark blue of a man's shirt.

He waited.

Two tense minutes passed, then a man stepped into clear sight. He was a lean, hard-bitten man of around thirty with a big black hat and sloping shoulders. There was a naked six-gun in his fist.

Setting the foresight squarely on the fellow's chest, Brazos lifted the backsights to frame the target. The man came forward a short distance, then stopped, head angling as his eyes peered this way and that. Finally he turned and called:

"All clear, Chad."

"Go check out them rocks!" came a gruff order from the scrub.

The man started forward and covered a further ten yards or so before Brazos' voice stopped him dead.

"Far enough, joker!"

The man froze, gaped, then did an extremely foolish thing. Catching the faint outline of a big head and shoulders, he lifted his gun and fired. The rifle jarred hard against Brazos' shoulder. His target's head snapped back and the man fell in a heap, his eyes staring sightlessly on either side of the small black hole between them.

Savage shouts sounded from the brush, followed by a volley of shots. Slugs lashed at Brazos' rock nest. Sliding down and back, the young giant made a speedy calculation. Half a dozen guns or more, he figured.

Out of reach of the guns below the rock rim, Brazos glanced over his shoulder to where his horse was cached in a rocky depression, then he jerked his head as the shooting abruptly ceased and a rough voice sounded.

"You up there! This is Chad Irons, you son-of-a-bitch!"

"Kinda figgered that," Brazos called back. He drew his powerful legs up beneath him, ready for the dash back to the horse.

"You killed one of my men, you murderin' bastard!"

"So?"

Irons, hunched at the base of a tall willow, bit down on his fury. "You!" he called. "You get into town and tell that dirty McCloud I'll give him until midnight to haul his freight. You hear that? Midnight or I'll wipe the whole dirty nest of you out, I swear it!"

Strung around Irons, the badmen waited tensely for a reply, but there wasn't one. All they heard was the swift drum of hoof beats as Hank Brazos' appaloosa carried him back to Redemption.

"Until midnight?" McCloud's voice was grave.

"That's what he said, Deacon," said Brazos.

"You going to accept the offer, Deacon?" asked Benedict.

McCloud grasped the gallery rail and drew himself up to his full height, his gaze sweeping around the town where the members of the Brethren stood armed and ready to defend their homes and their lives.

"Here we came," he said simply, "and here we stay!"

It was what they'd hoped he would say, but as they left the house some time later, Benedict and Brazos were aware of the tremendous odds; a bunch of out-laws against a town full of peaceful men.

Scanning the empty fields as they reached the street, Brazos said, "I wonder if Irons is as good as his word, Yank? I wonder if he means to give us until midnight, or is it just a trick to throw us off guard?"

"We'd better keep sharp," Benedict said.

"Rock of ages cleft for me
Let me hide myself in Thee ... "

The sounds of singing from the big white church came pure and clear on the cool night air as Duke Benedict and Hank Brazos patrolled the southern side of town. No lights showed in Redemption and the night was stiff with tension—but they could still sing.

The two tall men paused briefly to listen, then moved on towards the cow corrals where Brothers Smoke and Cassidy were posted. After several yards, Brazos drew up.

"Tell me somethin', Yank. If you was still wearin' your purty blue officer's uniform, and we was at Shiloh or Bull Run in a set-up like this, what would you do?"

"Why, I'd mount a detail and try to find the enemy camp, of course. Take the fight to the enemy—that is a cardinal rule of battle. Usually, that is."

"But you wouldn't do it here, eh?"

"Not wouldn't—couldn't." Benedict gestured at the darkness. "Without light, the odds would have to be on the enemy's side. The detail—and that would have to be you and me—would have no better than a two-to-one against chance of coming back." A pause, then: "That would leave just the Deacon and a lot of men who hardly know one end of a gun from the other."

"Yeah." Brazos sighed. "Reckon that's about how I figure it out."

They moved on again until a challenge came from the corrals. "Who's there?"

They identified themselves and Cassidy emerged from the gloom carrying a rifle. The man seemed ill at ease as he fiddled with the gun.

"Where's Smoke?" Benedict queried, peering about for the second sentry.

"Smoke? Why, he … er … he just went back for some coffee."

Cassidy was a lousy liar. This was so patently plain that both men were immediately suspicious.

"He was given orders not to quit his post, no matter what," Brazos growled, looking closely at the man. Suddenly the lie, Cassidy's nervousness, and the recollection of their violent set-to with Smoke at the Paradise Mine came together with a jolt that sent Brazos reaching, jaw out-thrust, for Brother Cassidy's collar. "He never went for no coffee, Cassidy," he said threateningly. "Where is the varmint? Come on, out with it afore I kick it out of you!"

Cassidy trembled as he tried to twist away from Brazos. But the bloody day had sapped what little iron the man had in him—and an unpleasant clash with Smoke not half an hour back had left him shaken badly.

"Leave me be, damn you, Brazos," Cassidy gasped. "I dunno where he's gone and I don't care what he's—"

The edge of Brazos' right hand chopped down, knocking Cassidy's hat loose. Crimson splashed and Cassidy swung blindly at Brazos' face. Brazos grunted and hit him again and then Benedict screwed the foresights of a Colt .45 into the man's ribs.

"There is definitely something fishy going on here, Cassidy," Benedict said icily. "Spill it or you're dead."

Cassidy was terrified now. "All right, all right," he bleated. "But I never done nothin'. I even told him I wouldn't go with him."

"Go where with him?" Brazos demanded, pushing Cassidy back against the corral corner post.

"To … to join up with Irons."

The two men stared. Brazos cocked a big fist, said, "Keep talkin'," and Cassidy got his tongue working again. Quickly.

"Charlie figgered we was done for here, so he went out to find Irons. He … he used to ride with him in the old days. He wanted me and Tarr to go with him, but Tarr wouldn't go and I run outa nerve at the last minute. I don't figure my chances too good here but I wasn't goin' out there to mebbe get shot down by Irons in the dark."

"The dirty Judas!" Brazos breathed. "I shoulda known that sly bastard wouldn't—"

"Never mind that," Benedict cut him off. "This could play our way, Reb. Cassidy, where was Smoke heading?"

"He never said, but he reckons he knew where he might find Irons. Somethin' about the old days ..."

They believed him. Cassidy was past lying.

"You been in with him all along, ain't you, Cassidy?" Brazos said. "You was in on stealin' the gold and all?" Cassidy nodded wearily and Brazos went on: "He kilt Jackson, didn't he? Come on, you lily-livered son of a bitch—it had to be him."

A last spark of resistance flickered in Cassidy and Brazos snuffed it out with a short, hard jolt to the belly.

"Yes!" Cassidy choked, sagging against the rails. "But don't tell Charlie I told you or he'll—"

"Shut your mouth," Benedict rapped. Then, turning to Brazos: "Damnation, Reb, this could have been our break. If we knew where Smoke went, we could have followed him and perhaps jumped the gang without—"

"Bullpup."

"What?"

Brazos' teeth flashed in an excited grin. "Bullpup can trace a billy goat through a cesspool, Yank. You know that."

"By Jupiter," Benedict breathed, turning to the darkness beyond the corrals. "If Smoke wasn't lying ... if he does know where Irons is camped ..." He turned back to Brazos. "But could that ugly hound do it?"

"With a pair of Smoke's boots to give him the scent he could," Brazos assured him, grabbing hold of the luckless Cassidy again. "And you're gonna come with me and get me a pair, ain't you, horseface?"

"He will," Benedict said as Cassidy made no attempt to resist. "All right, go get those boots, Reb. I'll stay here and hunt up someone more reliable to stand this lookout."

"Right," Brazos grunted, pushing Cassidy in front of him. "Let's go, horseface."

"And, Reb—"

"Yeah, Yank?"

"Bring two boxes of bullets, too."

"Got you."

"Chad. Hey, you there, Chad?"

Sprawled on his saddle blanket in the old Zuni Indian cave in the Sourdough Mountain foothills, Chad Irons stiffened as the sudden shout broke the night's stillness.

"What the—?" he gasped. Then, leaping to his feet, gun in hand: "Douse that goddamn light!"

Carson Bass squeezed out the candle and the cave where the outlaws were gathered, plunged into total darkness.

"Murch!" Irons yelled down to the sentry posted below. "Who the Sam Hill was that hollerin'?"

Before Murch could reply, the voice called again from the pine clump that shielded the cave. "Chad, it's me, Charlie Smoke. You remember me, Chad?"

"Smoke!" Irons said as his men grouped around him. "Show yourself, Smoke, real quick!"

Footsteps sounded in the gloom. There was a metallic click as Murch cocked his Winchester below. The footsteps halted, then a match burst into life and the torso and black-bearded face of Charlie Smoke jumped out of the blackness fifty feet away.

"See, Chad," he called. "It's me right enough!"

"You know this joker, Chad?" Carson Bass whispered at Irons' shoulder.

"Yeah, I know him. He was a good boy—once." Irons lifted his voice. "What's the play, Charlie?"

"I come to join you, Chad," Smoke called back as the match went out. "Wanted to this mornin' as soon as you rode in, but I had to bide my time." Another match flared and Smoke grinned. "Figured I'd find you here, Chad, on account of we used to camp here in the old days when we was huntin' grizzlies in the mountains. You remember, Chad?"

"Figure it's a trick, Chad?" breathed One-Shot Alf.

"Mebbe, mebbe not," replied Irons. "Carson, you and Alf git out there and comb them trees to make sure he ain't got company." He raised his voice. "Okay, Charlie, come on in and come in careful."

It was ten minutes before Bass and Alf returned to report that Smoke had come alone. By then, after talking with Smoke, Chad Irons had realized that Charlie Smoke knew him too well to try and cross him.

They relit the candle and Chad Irons' face was wearing a grin as he tossed big Smoke a bottle of rye. Then Smoke started to tell him about the set-up in Redemption.

The way Irons saw it, Smoke's defection from the enemy camp was just what they'd needed to boost their spirits and to give them valuable information on Redemption's defenses. It was a good omen.

Hank Brazos reached out a big hand and touched Bullpup's head. The dog immediately squatted and stared silently through the black trunks of the trees at the dim yellow glow in the cliff wall ahead.

After half an hour's walk on Bullpup's trail as his sure nose led them along Charlie Smoke's scent across the valley to the mountains, the eyes of the two men crouched on either side of the dog had grown fully accustomed to the darkness. They could see the dim shape of the sentry just a short way ahead, and they heard him clear his throat above the murmur of voices from above.

The clay wall in front of the cave that the Indians had built had crumbled away with time, leaving the cavern open. A dozen deep steps cut into the rock face led up to the cave.

The trail partners crouched there a full minute with guns in hands, taking in every detail of the scene before Duke Benedict turned to Brazos. In the faint glow of the light, Benedict's handsome features looked as if they were stamped from steel.

"You ready?" His voice was the softest whisper.

Brazos nodded his head silently and lifted his gun.

There was a hanging moment of silence and then Benedict's shout rang out:

"Irons! You're surrounded! Throw down your guns!"

Heads jerked around but bodies remained rooted, frozen with shock. Then the frozen moment was gone and the outlaws burst into action, slashing wildly for their guns as the candle blinked out and lookout Murch threw a rifle shot at the trees.

Benedict's guns flamed and big Murch, rustler, thief and woman-killer, died without knowing he'd been hit. Brazos' Colt stormed at the cavern and a red finger of death drove into Joe Pickett's skinny body and belted him into the wall. He was dead before he fell.

"You double-crossin' son of a bitch!" Chad Irons raged and blasted two shots into Charlie Smoke's big body at point-blank range.

The Zuni cave hadn't been chosen with defense in mind. The badmen who survived those first chaotic seconds were made brutally aware of that by the carnage going on around them, and with Irons showing the way, they leaped the ten feet to the ground, guns spitting as they fell.

Four men jumped from the cave and three hit the ground alive. Slowed by a wound he'd received seconds earlier and presenting a big target in the hellish light of his companions' gun flashes, Pat Quill took three slugs on the way down and didn't even feel the impact of his body on stone when he hit.

Irons, Bass and One-Shot Alf scurried away as they found ground, Bass fanning his six-gun with lethal skill and One-Shot concentrating solely on flight. Chad Irons, burning with murderous anger, took a gigantic leap through whistling slugs and found the cover of the blood-spattered rock where Murch had died.

His guns hot, Duke Benedict followed the fleeting figure of One-Shot Alf. Bullets smacked stone and rock chips screamed, then there was a dull thud as lead found flesh and One-Shot went cartwheeling into eternity.

A jagged scream lifted above the gun storm when Carson Bass took two slugs in the knee not an inch apart. He went down shooting. Seconds later, Brazos was hit by a bullet from Chad Irons' deadly gun.

The slug caught Brazos in the left shoulder, spinning him away from his tree cover and down a steep slope. Bullpup whimpered and dashed to his side as the Texan struggled to a sitting position. Emptying his right-hand gun at Irons' position, Benedict slewed around and dived down the slope to Brazos' side.

"Reb—you hit bad?"

"Hell, no," Brazos panted thickly, gunless right hand pressing against the wound. "I ain't near through with them yet."

Benedict pushed Brazos' hand away and traced the wound with his fingers as bullets continued to chop at the trees above them. The shoulder bone was intact, but the big man was bleeding freely. Too freely.

"We're leaving," he decided, reefing Brazos to his feet.

"Go?" Brazos was indignant. "Go where? We ain't through here yet."

"Quit while you're in front—a good gambler's gospel. Don't you understand?—we've whipped them, Reb. Two left alive and one of them hit hard."

"No, damnit," Brazos rasped, pulling free. "I tell you we can still—"

131

He broke off abruptly as a wave of dizziness hit him. He sagged heavily against Benedict, then shook his head. "You know, mebbe I do feel kinda puny at that ..."

Benedict didn't wait any longer. Throwing Brazos' right arm over his shoulder, he lumbered the big man through the trees. The guns had stopped behind them, but when they'd gone only a short distance, Benedict heard the sharp snap of a twig. Freeing himself from Brazos whose momentary weakness had passed, he pulled a gun free and emptied it into the trees where they'd made their stand.

Shots flared back, accompanied by a venomous curse from Chad Irons, snarling in the blackness like an enraged animal. Then they were moving away again, Bullpup finding the trail with his nose as Benedict covered their rear with his guns and Brazos trotted, his iron constitution already throwing off the shock of his wound.

TEN

THE CHALLENGE

From his balcony, Deacon Luther McCloud swept his gaze over the town and the rolling green and gold country beyond. It was high noon. Rain had fallen during the early hours of the morning, but now the hot sun was shining over Peaceful Valley, over a world washed clean by the rain.

Was Chad Irons lurking somewhere out there? the Deacon wondered. Was he licking his wounds and waiting for the chance to strike again? Or was he gone? There was no telling, but there wouldn't be any real rest for Redemption until he knew for sure, one way or the other.

Turning on his high black heels, McCloud walked back along the gallery to his open study doors and went in, his big Peacemaker Colt .45 jutting from the holster on his hip.

"All quiet?" Duke Benedict asked.

"All quiet." The Deacon sat down in his big carved chair and looked at the tall, slim man seated by the window. His black hair was meticulously brushed and his handsome face clean-shaven. Now, dressed in tight-fitting black trousers and a full-sleeved white silk shirt, Benedict looked much more like a professional gambler than a lethal gunfighter. But, after the bloody gun battle at the caves, the Deacon knew he was looking at one of the very top men in a deadly trade. Perhaps a man as good or better than himself.

An enigma, the Deacon told himself, leaning back in his chair. A man of conflicting strengths and weaknesses, a cynic in some ways, but also an idealist and a committed fighter for things he believed in. McCloud had already thanked Benedict and Hank Brazos profusely for what they'd done last night, and the wounded Brazos and the Brethren Elders had just left the Deacon's office five minutes ago, after the senior Brothers of Redemption had formally expressed their gratitude. Neither Benedict nor Brazos, McCloud had observed, had seemed comfortable while the plaudits were being handed out. McCloud, conscious of a growing bond between himself and Benedict, a man so much his opposite in many ways, hadn't been surprised when Benedict had elected to stay on after the others had gone. He was glad he had now, for he was just realizing that he hadn't asked the two tall men the most important question of all.

Why?

Duke Benedict ashed his cigar in a brass saucer and set it back between his white teeth when the Deacon put the question to him.

"Surely you can guess the answer to that yourself, Deacon."

"I suppose I have theories, knowing the goodness that lurks in the hearts of most men ... but no, I couldn't say I know the answer for sure."

"Self-preservation," Benedict said laconically. "Smoke's actions presented us with an opportunity to come to grips with Irons rather than wait until today, when Irons would surely have held the advantage. We simply took the opportunity when it presented itself."

McCloud nodded slowly, but he didn't believe Benedict. In his opinion, Benedict and Brazos had taken such terrible risks last night simply to protect the men, women and children of Redemption.

It was, he reflected, perhaps the most memorable example of practical Christianity he'd ever encountered and one he would never forget. But, aware that his opinion would embarrass Duke Benedict, who'd stated once that he was suspicious of Christianity, he didn't put his thoughts into words.

All he said was, "Well, I shall not touch on the incident again, Brother, except to say that Redemption will be forever in your debt."

"It could be a little premature to say Redemption has been saved, Deacon."

"You mean Irons, of course." McCloud frowned. "You believe we haven't seen the last of him?"

"I have a hunch we haven't." Benedict rose and came across to the desk. "Deacon, if Irons is still alive and in the valley, don't you think that now, while we're on top, we should mount a hunt for him?"

"No," McCloud said in a way that brooked no argument. "If he is out there, he will have to come to us."

"You think he will do that?"

"The man is a tiger, Brother Benedict. Tigers attack, they never flee."

"Then we just wait?"

"Yes, Brother … we just wait …"

The aroma that rose up to greet him when he pulled the cork from the jug was a rare perfume to Hank Brazos' nostrils. Just one whiff conjured up memories of gilded whisky palaces in Santa Fe, roaring drinking sprees in San Antone and Dallas, a hundred welcoming saloons and a thousand cherished hangovers.

"It's gotta be ready," he said. "It smells readier than anythin' I ever drunk in my natcherl."

"Just one more day, Hank," Joe Stecher insisted.

"One more day … one more day," Brazos mimicked, adjusting the calico sling binding his left arm. "You been sayin' that every day for a week. I tell you I need a drink now."

"Twenty-four hours," the old blacksmith said, replacing the cork, "and she'll be perfect."

"Look, you broken-winded old cracker, if it wasn't for me, you'd likely be planted six foot under by now with that dirty jug sittin' on top o' your grave sproutin' flowers." He tapped his wounded shoulder. "Look

136

at this. I got that fightin' fer the likes of you and your stupid jug. And now you won't even give a man a slug to ease the pain."

"Hank, it's on account of we all owe you so much that I got to say no. I ain't about to give no hero no moonshine of mine that ain't just perfect."

Brazos stared at him stonily. "Tell me somethin', old man? You ever had a jug busted over your baldy, speckled old head?"

Joe Stecher gave a gap-toothed grin. He knew the young giant was joking. At least he hoped he was.

"Tomorrow, Hank."

Chad Irons lay under a cottonwood in thick grass, the brim of his hat slanted against the afternoon sun. He was a mile from Redemption and he could see people moving on the streets. A burning cigarette dangled from his thin lips as he scratched his black beard stubble with the muzzle of his gun.

He was alone.

Three miles away, the bodies of good men who were to have been the nucleus of his outlaw empire, were bloating in the hot sun. Somewhere, far down the river trail to Wainright, Carson Bass, his best friend from Placerville, was riding south with all his nerve leaking out of a crippled leg. He hadn't even tried to talk Bass out of leaving. A man with no guts was no good to Chad Irons. To him, he wasn't a man at all.

Alone. One man against a town. The odds had looked impossible this morning as he'd sat brooding and licking his wounds, but then a plan had formed slowly in the dark corners of his brain. And it could work. It could work because Deacon McCloud was what he was. Preacher or no, McCloud had been a great gunfighter, and gunfighters never really change. Their great strength and their great weakness is their pride. Irons knew all about that, for the same pride spurred him on when almost any other man would take a calm look at the odds and ride off.

Coming to a sitting position, he took out the label of the sliced peaches can, on the back of which he'd written his note to McCloud. His lips moved as he read it again. Yes, it sounded just right. If McCloud could still be goaded, then this would do it.

He folded the paper, put it back in the pocket of his shirt and looked at the sky. About three hours to sunset. Clouds were working across from the north. If they built up, it would be dark tonight. Good.

He lay back on his elbows and stared down at the town again. After awhile he began to whistle through his teeth. The first thing he'd do when the town was his again, he decided, would be to put a goddamn match to that big white church.

"Everything all right, Gist?"

Leaning from the window of the house where he was standing watch on the north side of town, Brother Gist nodded his blond head. "Everythin' is quiet, Brother Benedict. How's the shoulder, Brother Brazos?"

"Mendin' fast. Keep sharp, Gist."

"Sure will."

The two men moved on, Bullpup swaggering ahead, on the lookout for cats.

"You should be resting with that shoulder," Duke Benedict said. "We can do without you tonight."

"Never was a great hand at restin' up, Yank. Besides, I can hardly feel her now. That Brother Miller sure knows a thing or two about patchin' up a bullet hole. Say, how you makin' out with that rosy-cheeked girl of his anyway?"

"Mind your own—" Benedict began, then stopped. "What's bothering your dog?"

Brazos looked ahead. Bullpup had stopped suddenly and, one paw lifted, was staring through the darkness towards Brother Cardiff's position by a tank stand. The hackles along the hound's spine were lifted and a low growl came from his throat.

"Somethin's wrong," Brazos whispered with sudden urgency, going into a crouch, his gun pointing at the dim bulk of the tank stand rising in the darkness. "Spread out, Yank."

Thirty feet apart, the two men crept forward, six-guns at the ready. At Brazos' side, Bullpup growled again. A dark shape was sprawled on the earth by the tank.

"Cardiff!" Benedict called.

No answer.

"Cover me," Benedict said. "I'll take a look."

Every tingling sense alert, Brazos watched Benedict's lean figure approach the form on the earth. Benedict bent and a low curse came from his lips.

"He's dead," he called back. "Let's scout."

They spent five minutes searching the area around the lookout's position before they were convinced that Cardiff's killer was gone. Returning grim-faced to the dead man, they found that he'd been stabbed through the heart. The murder knife was still embedded in his chest.

"Irons," Hank Brazos breathed. "It musta been—"

"There's something tied to the handle," Benedict cut him off as he pulled the Bowie knife free. "It's a note. Well, we can't do anything for Cardiff. Let's get back to Gist's house and see what this says."

Five minutes later they were in Brother Gist's front room with the shades drawn tight as Duke Benedict scanned the note.

"It was Irons right enough," he said thickly, gray eyes hard as chips of steel. "Listen to this."

He read:

"McCloud, You've took what is mine and I'm going to have it back. A lot of folks have got killed and a lot more will go the same way unless you got the guts to face me man to man. I am making you a proposition, McCloud. To save a lot more killing, I will meet you by the bridge at first light in the morning. If you kill me you win. If I kill you then your people quit my town. That means them two gunslingers of yours, too. I killed your kid brother and I can kill you, too, McCloud. You reckon God is on your side—well, be at the bridge by first light and we will see if he is or not. I spit on your God. Ring your bell at midnight if you agree, McCloud. If you don't, I will get all of you one by one. I swear it."

Benedict slowly lowered the paper. "It's signed by Chad Irons."

"He'll murder us all," skinny Brother Gist said in sudden panic. "Brother Benedict, Brother Brazos, what are we gonna do?"

"We're gonna see the Deacon," growled Brazos. "Pronto."

"But what'll I do?" Gist bleated. "What if he—"

"You'll stay here and you'll goddamn keep watch is what you'll do," Brazos said roughly. He headed for the door. "And while you're doin' it, see if you can't hunt up somethin' to use for a backbone."

The solemn chimes of the brass church bell rose clearly on the midnight air. The sounds seemed to linger for a moment above the rooftops before drifting away over the little creek and the sleeping fields, to finally fade into nothing as it was swallowed by the silence of the mountains.

"With all respect, Deacon McCloud," Duke Benedict said tightly, "you're a fool."

Standing tensely behind Duke Benedict and Hank Brazos in Deacon McCloud's study, Brothers Miller and Tucker stiffened at the insult, then looked apprehensively at the Deacon.

To their surprise, McCloud dismissed Benedict's accusation with a small smile. "Brother Benedict is a little overwrought, Brothers," he said. "We are all a little overwrought tonight."

Duke Benedict made a disgusted sound and reached for his cigar case. Having just spent a fruitless

141

hour trying to talk McCloud out of accepting Chad Irons' challenge, he felt depleted and angry.

As Benedict lit his cigar, Brother Miller stepped forward, clearing his throat. "Deacon, we might all be overwrought as you say, but I feel I must agree with Brothers Brazos and Benedict. You have no obligation to face this murderer in a—"

"Enough, Brother Miller," snapped McCloud, showing that he was prepared to take from Duke Benedict what he wouldn't from others. "I have made my decision and it will stand. Brothers Miller and Tucker, you are excused."

Flushing, Miller glanced at Benedict and Brazos, then nodded tight-lipped to Tucker and left.

"No pastor can afford to have his judgment challenged by his flock," said McCloud, standing tall and erect behind his desk when the door closed on the two men. "If he does, he is no longer the pastor."

"Why, Deacon?" Benedict asked. "Just tell me why you decided to face Irons."

McCloud looked surprised. "Why, because I must defend the safety of my flock, of course, Brother. What other reason could there be?"

"I believe I know the real reason," Benedict said quietly. "And I think Chad Irons guessed it, too—before he wrote that note. You claim to be a man of God, Deacon, and I believe you are. But there is still part of you that is a gunfighter. You still haven't come far enough to have the strength to turn down another man's challenge and not feel a coward because of it." Benedict's voice turned hard. "I don't believe you are going out there in the morning to protect your people. I believe you simply want to kill Chad Irons to prove to him and to the world that you are not afraid and that you're faster with a gun."

The Deacon's hawk face darkened as Benedict spoke. "Your concern for me is admirable, Brother," he warned, "but do not go too far. I accepted Irons' challenge to put an end to the killing ... because there is no other way."

"There *is* another way," Benedict said. "We can hunt Irons down and kill him." His voice turned reasonable. "Deacon, have you stopped to think what will happen if you lose?" He gestured. "All this, all you've built up—lost. Your people will be scattered to the four winds and Redemption will become an outlaw roost again for Irons and his scum."

"You speak as if you believe I might lose the battle, Brother," said McCloud. "I shall not. You yourself have witnessed my skill with a gun. With the Lord's help, I shall triumph against Satan."

Once again, Benedict felt admiration for Chad Irons' cleverness. The wording of the man's challenge to McCloud had made it difficult to refuse.

But he wasn't giving up yet. "Deacon, I know you are a fine pistol shot, perhaps as good as I've seen. But this is a gunfight where speed is at least as important as accuracy. It is a young man's profession, Deacon."

McCloud bridled. "I have the speed I always possessed, Brother."

"How do you know? How long since you faced a fast man?" Before the other could answer, Benedict pulled his right-hand gun and placed it squarely in the middle of McCloud's desk. Then, with McCloud and Brazos staring in puzzlement, Benedict stepped back, hands at his sides.

"Speed is what we are talking about, Deacon," he said. "You and I stand at an equal distance from that gun. Let us presume we are to fight and the man who can snatch up that gun first will win."

McCloud made a gesture of dismissal, but then, feeling Benedict's challenge, changed his mind. "Very well, Brother Benedict. However, I feel that games have no relation to reality in this deadly business."

"We shall see," said Benedict. "Brazos, give a signal."

Brazos shrugged, waited three seconds, then snapped his fingers. Two fast hands reached for the gun on the desk, which seemed to jump into Benedict's fist and was cocked and pointed inches from an astonished McCloud's face.

Benedict slowly straightened, palming the gun into leather. "A young man's game, Deacon …"

The Deacon was impressed, but in no way convinced. "Exercises, Brother Benedict," he said, tossing back a long lock of hair that had tumbled across his face. "When two men face each other and death is standing in the wings, it is courage and conviction that carry the day."

"Then there's no changing your mind?" said Brazos.

"None," smiled the Deacon, shaking his head. "But let me say that I know that your attempts to alter my will, spring from what I truly believe has become deep loyalty and affection for me, and I shall not forget it. Now, however, the hour grows late, Brothers, and I must pray and prepare. Goodnight to you both … and do not look so sober. Tomorrow there shall be singing and rejoicing amongst us, and the evil blight Satan has sent will have been purged and gone forever."

"Hell, will you light some place, Yank?" Brazos complained. "I'm gettin' tuckered out just watchin' you walk up and down."

Benedict went right on pacing to and fro across the parlor of Brazos' cabin, locked in a private battle between his common sense gospel of always looking out for number one and a crazy idea he'd hatched that just wouldn't go away.

Joe Stecher, who'd come to Brazos' house when he'd seen the two men return from McCloud's an hour back, was getting weary watching Benedict, too. With the word of what was going to happen at first light broadcast all over Redemption and keeping the whole town awake, Stecher had come over to find out if the Deacon still meant to face Chad Irons. Stecher was just as glum about the prospect as they were, but he didn't see what all Benedict's stamping up and down was going to achieve.

"No point in frettin' too much," the old man offered after a silence broken only by the sound of boot heels. "The old Deacon's no slouch when it comes to gunplay, you know, Duke. I reckon he'll beat Irons."

"So do I," said Brazos, though he didn't really mean it—not after having seen the ferocious Irons in action at the Zuni caves. But he was weary, his shoulder was aching, and he was ready to turn in. "He's bound to fight, so let him fight, Yank."

"He's not going to fight," Benedict said with sudden decision, and spinning on his heel, went out.

"Now what in the hell did he mean by that?" Joe Stecher said in puzzlement.

"How the hell would I know?" Brazos growled, getting up and going to the doorway. "He don't hardly never tell me nothin'."

ELEVEN

SINNERS, SAINTS AND SIX-GUNS

Sister Susie answered the door to Benedict's knock. Dark hair framed the pale oval of her face as she looked up at him in astonishment.

"Duke! What are you doing here at this hour?"

"Sorry, but there's something I need that can't wait, Susie."

Sister Susie blushed in the dark. "Why, Duke Benedict, you're an impossible man!"

"You misunderstand, Susie. I want a wig."

"A *what?*"

"A wig. Do you have one?"

The girl started to smile, then realized he was serious, "Why, no, I don't, Duke. But Sister Randolph next door has one. What on earth do you want with a—"

"Will you borrow it for me, Susie? There's a good girl."

"Well … well, all right, Duke. I'll get my robe."

The girl went inside the house, returning a minute later tying her robe about her slim waist. "It might take me awhile to wake Sister Randolph, Duke. You can wait inside if you wish."

Benedict smiled. "Thanks, Susie, but I'm sure your father wouldn't approve."

"Father isn't here. Brother Doherty has taken ill and father said he will have to sit up with him all night."

"Well, in that case …"

Seated in the gloom of the front room on the big plush sofa that he'd rested on one eventful night before, Duke Benedict lit a fresh cigar and waited for Susie to return. Now that the decision had been made, there could be no turning back, yet he couldn't help smiling. What was he trying to do? Was it possible that some of the brotherly love that was to be had by the peck around here had rubbed off on him? That had to be the craziest possibility of all time.

Soft footsteps sounded ten minutes later and Sister Susie appeared as a dim silhouette in the doorway.

"Duke?"

"Here, Susie. Did you get it?"

She came across to him and in the darkness he was conscious of her sweet feminine smell. "Yes," she said, passing him a dark object. "Sister Randolph was terribly curious about why I wanted it, but I told her

I couldn't sleep and wanted to try out a new way of dressing my hair."

"I won't forget this, Susie," he said, setting the wig aside and stubbing out his cigar.

She brushed against him then. It might have been accidental or it might have been deliberate. Whatever it was, the feel of her soft body against his sent an electric shock running through him. He was surprised— not because Sister Susie was not a very desirable young girl but because, until that touch, he'd been totally preoccupied with what he had to do. Now he realized that daybreak was still a long way off ... that tomorrow loomed uncertain before him ...

His arms went around her waist. She drew closer and her breathing suddenly grew heavy. Her hands went through his hair as his hands moved over her waist. She spoke his name in a whisper, then sank to her knees before him. He felt the heavy swell of a breast against his cheek as she fumbled with her robe. He ran his hands along her body inside the opened robe and he had never felt anything so smooth beneath his hands.

Suddenly she stiffened. "Duke ... Duke, this isn't right. But ... but it could be right ..."

"What do you mean, Susie?" It felt right to Benedict.

"We could ask the Deacon to marry us, Duke. Then everything would be all right. Please, Duke, couldn't ...?"

Benedict sighed, released her, reached for his cigar again and got to his feet. That old word marriage again. It was a black night all around and no mistake.

A rooster crowed, flapped his wings and strutted.

Redemption's rooftops emerged slowly from the darkness. Again the rooster crowed. All through town, lamps burned behind shutters and shades. Few had found the comfort of sleep in Peaceful Valley this long night.

The rooster crowed a third time and the door of the Deacon's study opened.

He stood in the doorway, tall and calm looking. He didn't seem surprised to find Duke Benedict standing leaning lazily against the big open east window of the parlor, the burning end of a cigar glowing in his hand.

"First light, Brother Benedict."

"Yes, Deacon, first light …"

Soft lamplight gleamed on the polished black gun rig buckled around the Deacon's hips as he came across to the window. He was clean-shaven, and his mane of black hair shone from brushing. He breathed deeply as the cool morning air trembled the drapes. Benedict saw his hands. They looked steady.

"Has he come?" the Deacon asked.

"Not yet."

McCloud peered out and saw figures moving in the mist below. The members of his Brethren were gathering to either rejoice or lament. He nodded his head slowly, then turned back to Benedict with a quizzical look.

"No more pleas or arguments, Brother?"

"I used them all up last night."

"Yes, I suppose you did." McCloud sighed reflectively. "It has been a long night, Brother, and a revealing one for me." He lifted his hands. "A man changes. Once the deadliness of these hands was all that mattered to me. Now I realize they are merely tools with which I shall defend my life." His hands dropped and he looked directly at Benedict. "I thought it would be different when I faced my brother's killer, Brother Benedict, but there is no thirst for vengeance in me today. I shall slay Chad Irons, but triumph will not be there. Strange, is it not?"

Benedict's black-lashed eyes were shadowed. "Not to me. You might have been a killer once, Deacon, but not anymore."

"Yet I shall kill ..."

McCloud stopped and stiffened. A slow thud of hoof beats had sounded from beyond the town. He and Benedict looked out, and in the strengthening light that probed the mist tatters hanging in the morning air, saw a solitary horseman riding the trail from the east.

A sound went through Redemption. It could have been a gust of wind, it could have been the town catching its breath.

"He has come," the Deacon said. He turned to Benedict and extended his hand. "Just in case the Lord should frown on my cause, Brother. We tread different paths, but there is much in it that is the same."

"Indeed there is."

151

Their hands clasped, and then the Deacon squared his shoulders and turned away. "Enough of words," he said. "Let the guns say what is left to be said."

"They will, Deacon," said Duke Benedict, and, whipping out his Colt, lifted it high and brought the barrel crashing down on the Deacon's head.

"Where the hell is Benedict?" growled Hank Brazos, standing in the chill street before the crowd of men on the store porch, his blue eyes watching the solitary figure standing in the thin fog a hundred yards distant.

Nobody knew.

"I seen him headin' for the Deacon's house, Brother Brazos," a black-garbed Brother replied. "But that was a long time—"

The man broke off at the sound of boot heels and Brazos turned his big head to see Deacon McCloud's tall figure emerge from the alley beside his house, and, not even glancing their way, head towards the solitary figure along by the bridge.

"A prayer for the Deacon," Brother Miller said, and clasped his hands.

"He'll likely need all of that backin' he can get," Hank Brazos muttered bitterly. He still couldn't figure where the Yank had got to. He wished he were here—if for no other reason than to reassure him that the Deacon wasn't going to get himself killed deader than a bull-tromped wolf.

It had deceived them; it would deceive Chad Irons.

Duke Benedict was certain of that now as, dressed in the Deacon's high black boots, flowing frock coat and with Sister Randolph's long black wig curling around his shoulders from beneath one of the Deacon's tall black hats, he left the last of the towners behind and walked towards the bridge.

Irons looked impressive, standing wide-legged and unmoving in the dead center of the street. Only a man supremely self-confident could stand there so rock steady, ready to face a man as formidable as the Deacon.

The old familiar tension was there inside Benedict as he halted fifty feet from the man he had to kill. The killer looked tanned and strong in the eerie light with the pink flush of day staining the sky behind him and the ghostly wraiths of fog misting between them. All Peaceful Valley was quiet.

"You don't look quite so tall as I recall, McCloud," Irons said.

Benedict didn't reply. He didn't know if Irons could recognize the Deacon's voice, but he wasn't taking any chances. The disguise had worked so far and it must go on working until this was over. He moved the panel of the frock coat to reveal the thonged gun riding his hip.

The gesture was not wasted on Chad Irons. A thin, cruel grin worked over his face. He moved his feet a little, crouching to present a smaller target. His hand hovered over his gun.

"When you are ready, preacher man."

Benedict didn't speak, didn't move. He could feel all the silent eyes of the people of Redemption on his back. He was acutely aware of all the sounds and smells of the new morning.

Then Irons went for his gun. Benedict's right hand blurred and his matchless reflexes ripped his lead-spewing Peacemaker up in a blue blur and he sent rolling thunder crashing down the street. Twice he fired, then he holstered the gun. His hand was clear of the gun before Chad Irons fell dead on his back, his bullet-holed Stetson rolling slowly in the dirt behind him.

Down the street they cheered as the tall figure with the flowing mane turned and started walking slowly back towards them. The cheering was taken up by everybody except big Hank Brazos, who, with a feeling of unreality, was staring up at the gallery of Deacon McCloud's house where McCloud stood clutching the railing.

The others suddenly grew aware of McCloud and the cheering broke off as if a switch had been thrown. Bewildered faces stared up at the silent Deacon, then turned in confusion to see the "other" Deacon McCloud taking off hat and wig.

"Benedict!" Brazos gasped. "Goddamnit, I thought there was somethin' familiar about that gunplay. What the tarnal is this?"

Benedict didn't answer. His face was drawn and pale from what he'd had to do. The hat and wig in his hand, he stopped in the center of the street and looked up at the balcony of McCloud's house.

"I'm sorry, Deacon," he said. "But he would have killed you."

Standing at Benedict's side now, Brazos stared up at McCloud and waited for the thunderbolt. It didn't come. Dazed with pain, McCloud had lurched out onto the gallery just seconds before the gunfight exploded, and had seen the incredible speed of both victor and vanquished. This had hammered reality home.

"I know," he said. "I would be lying dead if you hadn't taken my place, Brother Benedict."

Some of the color came back to Benedict's cheeks at that, for he too had expected a thunderbolt.

"A young man's game, Deacon," he said quietly. "And definitely not a game for men of God ..."

"But I still don't figger why," Hank Brazos muttered in puzzlement an hour later when the excitement was beginning to die down and the two men left McCloud's house. "Why'd you stick your neck out that way?"

"Nothing complicated," Benedict said. He brushed a hand against his gun. "Mainly curiosity, I suppose ... I wanted to see just how good Irons was."

"And no other reason?"

"None."

"You're a liar."

"I've been called that before," Benedict said with a mocking smile and sauntered off. Watching him go, Hank Brazos wondered if one man ever really got to know another. He knew damned well that Benedict had put his life on the line for McCloud, but such a thing was so out of character for Duke Benedict

155

that it made the big Texan's head ache just thinking about it.

Brazos' head was still aching ten minutes later as he loafed about town. Then he remembered the jug. He propped as if divine inspiration had struck him. If ever he needed a drink, it was now—and Joe had promised that the jug would be ready by today …

Men and women stopped to stare curiously after the big form of Hank Brazos as he headed at a trot for Joe Stecher's house. He burst through the front door without knocking and shouted Stecher's name—then came to a frozen halt. Old Joe was sitting on a bench with his head in his hands. At his feet on the floor lay the shattered remains of a familiar gray jug and a vast dark stain.

"Joe!" Brazos' voice caught in his throat. "Joe, that ain't—"

"I'm sorry, Hank," the old man said, getting up. "But … but after the gunfight, I was so het up, I scooted back here to get a drink ready for you and me and Duke and I … I … well, I guess I was shakin' …"

Hank Brazos' jaw seemed to fall a good three inches. His eyes grew glassy. The fragrant, heady, unbearably delicious aroma of totally matured sage juice was thick enough to hang your hat on. His tongue, dry as a piece of corned jerky, rasped around his teeth. Then his big, rocky, hanging jaw shook a little and skinny little Joe Stecher turned away, frightened that he'd have to witness the enormous spectacle of two hundred and twenty pounds of teak-tough Texan breaking into tears.

The goodbyes were over and they rode slowly away from the tiny town on a morning gold with sunlight and rich with the sweet, pure smells of the wild. The good people of Redemption had begged Benedict and Brazos to stay on, but the trail was calling. Their horses were frisky after their long idleness on the best of fodder; and Bullpup, sensing the long miles and the changing scenes ahead, scampered before them through the lush grass.

They rode a mile to a timbered hill, reined in and looked back. Tiny, black-garbed figures stood against the yellow of the street, kerchiefs fluttering in little banners of color.

Silence held the two for long minutes, each lost in his own private thoughts. Then Brazos let out a windy sigh and shook his big head. Forgetting his thirst for the moment, he said quietly, "Funny ain't it, Yank ... when we hit this valley, I figured all of them, the Deacon tossed in, was kinda tetched with all that theein' and thouin' and offerin' everythin' up to the Lord. But now, hell ... I just don't know. You reckon they might have somethin', Yank? Somethin' ordinary folks don't have?"

Benedict's gray eyes were thoughtful. After a silence, he said, "Perhaps they do, Reb." Another pause, then: "I know one thing, perhaps more clearly than I ever did before. There's cold comfort in atheism."

Brazos' brow furrowed. "What's atheism, Yank?"

Benedict smiled. "Why, it's nothing, Reb ... just nothing at all."

They were hanging from the lamps when Benedict and Brazos, dusty, hot and dry as a powder house in Death Valley, tied up outside Wainright's Trail End Saloon the following night.

It was pay night in Wainright, and they were in from the Box 40, the Triangle T, Jingle Bob Creek and even as far distant as Mule Mesa Ranch on the border. Every table was full, the faro layouts were roaring, and it was ten deep around the bar where Blind Billy Hogg, Big-Chested Daphne and four Saturday night barkeepers were dispensing beer, whisky and old Juniper Gin with furious speed.

"God's teeth!" Benedict groaned in frustration, almost as badly in need of alcoholic sustenance as Brazos now that the blood and violence of Peaceful Valley were behind them. "This is hopeless."

"Not a bit of it, Yank."

"Of course it is ... and what in the name of Plato are you shoving me for?"

"Why, I just want for you to step aside a minute, Yank," Brazos said amiably. "You'll see why in a minute."

A drunk was slobbering and muttering on a chair nearby. Too tired to really care, Benedict nevertheless watched with some curiosity as Brazos jerked the chair from under his rump, booted him aside, then jumped onto the chair to suck in a breath that swelled his barrel chest.

"Fire!" Brazos shouted.

Instant silence. A hundred heads twisted as one to see a great big stranger who looked like he wouldn't be scared to meet Old Scratch himself on a dark night, standing on a chair by the door wearing a look of total, spine-chilling panic.

"Fire!" he bellowed, twice as loud and twice as terrifyingly as before. "Fire, goddamnit, fire!"

There was just one further second of total, clock-stopping silence before the drunk Brazos had de-chaired bounded up, screamed "Fire" just once and went through the batwings like a runaway loco.

That started it. In an instant, one hundred men were stampeding for the doors in panic. Dusty Joe Dunbar, who'd been propping around on crutches for at least five years and maybe longer, was first out, overtaking and clearly outstripping two superbly fit young punchers from the Jingle Bob Ranch.

"What's burnin'?" screamed Beef Duckett tramping eighty-year-old Tucker Greathouse into the boards as he charged through the back door. "Where?"

"The whole God-awful town!" shrieked Panhandle Bob the blacksmith, taking one of the batwings with him as he crashed out.

They went through the doors and they went through the windows. Flat Jack Smith beat the press by leaping up on a table and then running nimbly over the packed heads and shoulders, while Mick Mok the storekeeper clambered onto the bar, dived ten feet to catch a chandelier, swung like a circus high wire artist and launched himself spectacularly through the main front window in a magnificent burst of exploding glass.

Then silence.

Duke Benedict's ice-cold nerve was famous in some quarters, but right at that moment he looked noticeably shaken as his eyes swept over the dust-filled, shattered saloon, to finally come to rest accusingly on the big man who was jumping down off the table looking totally pleased with his handiwork.

"You've lost your mind," Benedict gasped at length. "I've always known you were none too bright at best, but this … this …" Words failed him.

"Not at all, Yank," Brazos grinned, sauntering for the bar. "All I said was that there was a fire, and that's sure enough the truth."

Benedict strode after him, outraged in every inch. "Where?" he demanded. "Where's the fire, you misbegotten Texas moron?"

Unfazed, Brazos reached the bar, swept up an untouched jug of beer, smacked his lips and held it up for the light to shine through its cool amber depths before emptying it with one mighty gulp. Then, smacking his lips, he executed the wink of a happy man and belched shatteringly.

"Sure puts the old fire out, Yank."